SUMMER
GIRLS

Also by Hailey Abbott

SUMMER BOYS SERIES

SUMMER BOYS

NEXT SUMMER

AFTER SUMMER

LAST SUMMER

• • •

GETTING LOST WITH BOYS

WAKING UP TO BOYS

THE SECRETS OF BOYS

THE PERFECT BOY

FORBIDDEN BOY

THE OTHER BOY

FLIRTING WITH BOYS

BOY CRAZY

SUMMER
GIRLS

HAILEY ABBOTT

Point

New York Toronto London Auckland Sydney
Mexico City New Delhi Hong Kong Buenos Aires

No part of this publication may be reproduced, stored in a retrieval
system, or transmitted in any form or by any means, electronic,
mechanical, photocopying, recording, or otherwise, without written
permission of the publisher. For information regarding permission, write
to Scholastic Inc., Attention: Permissions Department, 557 Broadway,
New York, NY 10012.

Library of Congress Cataloging-in-Publication Data

Abbott, Hailey.
   Summer girls / by Hailey Abbott.
      p. cm.
   Summary: Cousins Jessica, Lara, and Greer, aged fifteen to sixteen, approach their family summer at a Maine beach cottage with
very different attitudes, but all look forward to meeting new boys
and having some fun.
   ISBN-13: 978-0-545-10268-1 (alk. paper)
   ISBN-10: 0-545-10268-5 (alk. paper)
   (1. Dating (Social customs)—Fiction.   2. Cousins—Fiction.
3. Friendship—Fiction.   4. Beaches—Fiction.   5. Maine—Fiction.)
I. Title.

PZ7.A149Sum 2009
(Fic)—dc22

2008043494

Copyright © 2009 by Alloy Entertainment
All rights reserved. Published by Scholastic Inc.

alloyentertainment
Produced by Alloy Entertainment
151 West 26th Street
New York, NY 10001

SCHOLASTIC, POINT, and associated logos are trademarks
and/or registered trademarks of Scholastic Inc.

Text design by Steve Scott
The text type was set in Bulmer.

12 11 10 9 8 7 6 5 4 3 2 1   9 10 11 12 13 14/0

Printed in the U.S.A. 40
First printing, May 2009

For my parents

1

Get Ready for the Hottest Summer of Your Life!

Jessica Tuttle glanced down at the cover of the June *Allure* as her parents' packed station wagon exited the Maine highway. The neon-pink headline had caught her attention at a gas station mini-mart somewhere along I-95, and although she wasn't in the habit of reading girly magazines, she'd had to pick this one up. Those nine tantalizing words summed up her entire goal for the next three months, as if the editors had magically read her mind. And even if the accompanying article suggested that the perfect summer hinged on collecting a wide range of tropical-colored eye shadows, it was still a very good sign.

"Mind if I take the scenic route, Jessi?" her father asked

from the driver's seat. "Let's see how much the town's changed."

She quickly rolled down her window as they reached Pebble Beach's Shore Boulevard, the salty ocean air sweeping into the car. The roadside forest had given way to cute shops and restaurants, and happy-looking tourists ambled up and down the wide sidewalks. Jessica excitedly craned her neck out the window and spotted the Lookout Diner and Ahoy Grill, two of the local landmarks that her older cousins had taken her to when she was a kid.

She drew a sharp breath as the ocean finally came into view. It had been three summers since she'd seen that beach, and now they were finally back. She'd practically grown up on this sandy shore, with her huge, extended family renting out the same three oceanfront cottages every summer since she could remember. But three years ago, one of the cottages had burned down in an electrical fire, putting an end to Jessica's favorite Tuttle tradition.

Since the fire, Jessica's parents had sent her to sports camps — first basketball, then swimming and softball. While she loved being surrounded by other athletes, summer had just felt so *wrong* anywhere else, especially with her big brothers, Jordan and Drew, working and her parents traveling. When the owner of the cottages had called in the spring to announce that the summer properties were available again, all of her aunts and uncles had jumped at the chance to revive their summer tradition.

Her father pulled the car to a stop, and Jessica could hardly believe her eyes.

"Not bad, huh?" her mom asked, adjusting the brim of her sunhat to get a better view.

"Oh. My. God!" Jessica squealed as she tumbled out of the car.

The rustic cottages from her childhood were gone. In their place were three ultramodern, stark-white structures with enormous, glittering windows. Around the back, a massive deck overlooked the water, with white umbrellas casting shadows over teak lounge chairs and a long table. The three houses shared a lawn and a driveway that spread out in front of her like a massive stone welcome mat. Now *this* was a summer home.

There were a couple of cars in the driveway, which meant that some other family members had arrived and were settling in. Jessica's mom unlocked the door to the one house that still looked empty.

As they carried their bags inside, Jessica took in the streamlined taupe couches and chairs scattered around the living room and the enormous plasma TV hanging over the granite fireplace.

"Love, love, *love!*" she shouted happily as she collapsed on a leather chaise. How could she *not* have an epic summer living in a house that looked like it was flown in straight from Malibu? She only wished she could see her brothers' reactions to the new houses, but Jordan was working at a camp a few towns away, and Drew was driving his own car up from Ithaca. Depending on when he woke up that morning, he could show up anytime between later today and the end of August.

Jessica wandered out to the deck, pulling her tank top over her head and adjusting her navy-blue polka-dot bikini. The large grill and canvas lounge chairs were new, but the wide-open view of the ocean was reassuringly familiar. This was the place she'd been dreaming about. The place where her older cousins had so many adventures. As she looked down to the pier in the distance, memories came flooding back — going to the pier with her cousins for ice cream, listening to their crazy conversations. The older cousins would be the only thing missing from this summer. Wild Ella, who Jessica once thought was like a real-life Barbie doll, and sensitive Jamie, who used to read to Jessica for hours, were in college and doing cool-sounding summer programs. Sporty Beth and supersmart Kelsi had graduated and had moved to New York and Boston to start their careers.

Jessica turned and let the gusty wind whip her pale blonde hair away from her face. She smiled, recalling the girls' infectious laughter and whispered gossip — and the countless boys who had hovered around them at all times. Wherever they were and whatever they did, they always seemed to be having the best times of their lives. She'd been so jealous when they'd slip out after family dinners. A few times she'd sat in her bedroom window and watched for them to come home, wishing that they'd take her along the next night.

And now it's my turn. Jessica smiled to herself. *I mean,* our *turn.*

Her cousin Greer from New York City and Uncle Mike's new stepdaughter, Lara, were going to be her summer roommates. Jessica didn't know Greer that well, since her parents rarely came to family functions, and she'd only met Lara at Uncle Mike's wedding last year. But Jessica already knew the three of them were going to rule Pebble Beach — which definitely meant meeting some Pebble Beach boys.

And, then, there they were.

Like out of a cheesy Kate Hudson movie, two deeply tanned, gorgeous boys stepped out from the shaded aisle between houses, both wearing shorts and no shirts, looking like they belonged in an Abercrombie catalog. Both guys had the same longish wavy brown hair with ends that had turned golden from the sun. When they saw her, they set down the Jet Ski they'd been lugging between them.

"Hey," said the slightly taller one. He looked about seventeen. "You must be one of the renters. I'm Liam."

5

Jessica nodded, already feeling shy.

"Connor," the younger-looking one said with a friendly smile. "Our dad owns the property. We're just moving this Jet Ski out of the garage."

"I'm Jessi — uh, Jessica," she corrected impulsively. Time to let her little-girl nickname die a quick death. She took a tiny, nervous step away, twisting a long strand of blonde hair around her finger.

"How do you like your new place?" Liam asked, grinning up at her. His confident smile made him even hotter, if that was possible. She was officially entranced.

"I love it," she replied honestly.

Connor spoke up. "We helped build them — the houses."

Liam swiftly punched his younger brother in the arm. "You helped what?" he asked sarcastically. "As I recall, all you helped with was calling for break time."

Connor shrugged gamely. "Yeah, well, unlike you, I'm still young. I need my rest." Connor dodged as Liam punched at him again and missed. "In your face!" Connor hooted while striking a dorky victory pose. Jessica couldn't help laughing, though Liam just shook his head, evidently used to his brother's goofiness. Connor turned back to Jessica. "If you ever need anything . . . I mean — with the house, let us know."

"Thanks, I will. I can't believe how much I missed this place." Jessica smiled at a familiar poplar tree in the far left corner of the yard. She let a seagull flying toward the horizon distract her from the boys' undeniable hotness. It gave her a chance to get her racing heart back under control.

Liam cleared his throat. "Do you have big plans for the summer?" he asked.

"Actually, I need to train for fall lacrosse tryouts." Jessica gestured at her gym bag, which her father had left near the deck doors. "I'm trying to make varsity, but it's been four years since a sophomore's done it."

Connor brightened. "We should practice together. I've got an old stick in the garage."

"Really? That'd be great! I was just going to try it alone, but having someone around is so much better." She paused, glancing out at the grassy yard. "The lawn isn't huge, but it's big enough for passing around," Jessica offered, then realized that probably sounded rude. "Oops, I mean — it's not small. At all. I —"

Connor shook his head ruefully. "I'll overlook that insult to our family's pride and joy. I'm free tomorrow, if —"

Liam cut in deftly. "So what are you up to tonight?"

Jessica turned to him, and shrugged. "Not sure. Anything going on?"

"Bonfire," Liam mentioned, nodding toward the beach. "You should come by."

The summer kickoff! "Okay," Jessica said, trying to hide her excitement. She'd been in Pebble Beach for less than ten minutes and she'd already met two cute guys and gotten an invite to the first party of the summer.

"Great. I'll look for you." Liam smiled steadily at her, his hair falling into his hazel eyes. With his sun-bleached hair and lean swimmer's body, it was like he'd walked straight out of her daydream.

Heat rose from Jessica's chest and up to her face. She broke away from his stare and looked down at her toenails. The clear polish was starting to chip.

As the boys picked up the Jet Ski and carried it through the gate and onto the beach, Jessica looked up and watched them. She thought of the copy of *Allure* and grinned. The hottest summer of her life had officially begun.

2

Lara Pressman stood on the toes of her scuffed silver flats and peered through the window of Sol, one of the small boutiques lining Shore Boulevard. Behind the HELP WANTED sign in the window, mannequins were posed in overpriced boho-chic beach clothes, artfully arranged to look disheveled. It reminded her of *US Weekly* pictures of celebrity spawn. The paparazzi-readiness turned her stomach. Lara was more of a vintage-store-tees kind of girl, but desperation moved her to push open the door.

"May I help you?" asked a redhead in a peasant top.

"Ten percent off this rack!" yelled a brunette with an unflattering middle part in her hair.

"I've got the *perfect* top to go with those gorgeous eyes!" a tall blonde practically screamed at her.

Like a cornered rabbit, Lara backed up until she felt the door behind her. She suddenly became conscious of how completely out of place she must look, in her old denim cut-offs and a white puffed-sleeve shirt with pin-tucked ruffles that she'd scored at a vintage shop on Damen Avenue in Chicago. Everything here smelled new and *rich*.

"Oops! Wrong turn — I was looking for the bakery!" She slipped back out the door, feeling the disappointed stares of the women working on commission.

She continued down the cobblestone street, taking in the weathered storefronts. If she had to leave Chicago for the summer, she supposed she could get used to this place. She, her mom, and her stepdad had arrived early that morning, before any of the others, and Lara hadn't bothered to settle in before coming into town. Now that she was fully awake, she could appreciate the beauty. The air smelled like salt-water taffy and the sky was a clear, bracing blue. Behind the local fudge shop, small sailboats and skimmers bobbed up and down in the local marina.

She also had to admit it was nice to see her mother so happy with her new husband, Mike Tuttle. Even if Lara had seen her in that blissful newlywed state once or twice — or five times — before. Really, who was counting?

As Lara cataloged her mom's failed marriages (technically it was only four, but counting the broken engagement brought it up to a whole hand's worth), she checked out the surf shop, record store, and florist, but they all wanted experienced help. When she spotted the SERVERS NEEDED sign in the window of Ahoy Grill, she perked up. Her stepdad had mentioned the great burgers at Ahoy, and she'd waited tables before. It would be tiring being on her feet all day, but she could rake in a lot of tips.

She smoothed down her short, pixie-cut black hair before approaching the redheaded hostess, who looked about her age. The hostess went to get the manager, and Lara checked out the red vinyl booths and brown paneling. The patrons in the booths were chowing down on typical diner fare, but the jukebox and tiny dance floor in the back hinted at a nightlife scene.

A man emerged through the kitchen door, his blue eyes appraising her shrewdly.

"I'm the manager here. Name's Richard," he said with an Australian drawl. "How can I help you?"

Lara held out her hand. "I'm Lara Pressman. I'd like to apply for the job."

Richard laughed as he shook her hand. "When it rains, it pours," he said. "Let's make it a double interview." He cocked his head in the direction of a booth in the corner. A dark-haired boy was sitting there, filling out an application. Lara sat down next to the stranger as Richard slid into the seat opposite them. Lara smiled cheerfully as he handed her a form. She needed this job way too much to let someone else steal it from under her. She filled out the application swiftly, handing it to the manager well before the boy did.

"All right," Richard began, looking over the forms. "Had a couple servers bail last week, so we're short-staffed this summer. I need at least two waiters, able to work all shifts. I'd need you to start right away. How does that sound so far?" He eyed them inquisitively.

"Perfect," Lara pronounced. The boy nodded. She stole a peek at her potential coworker while Richard shuffled papers around. Tall and thin, with longish dark hair, wearing a worn but clean Daniel Johnston T-shirt and faded jeans. Cute. The object of her stare glanced up, caught her eye, and smiled. She flushed and looked away.

Richard peered at her application. "Lara, is it? Looks like you have some experience."

"Right, um, I worked at a diner last summer." Lara wasn't nervous, but it was disconcerting to have the cute guy listening to her try to brag.

"And how'd you like it?"

"Considering that the one edible dish was pot roast, it wasn't too bad." Lara laughed at the memory. She'd planned on going to Interlochen Art Camp in Michigan, but when her mom's fourth divorce was finalized in May, Lara had decided to stay in Chicago for moral support. Then her mom had met Mike in August, and Lara split her time between watching Katharine Hepburn movies at home and doling out red meat to appreciative construction workers. "I just ended up serving a thousand pot roasts and watching the kitchen staff smirk at the occasional bad call by someone who didn't know any better."

Her fellow interviewee snickered and Richard smiled. "Well, our menu is a little more extensive than that," he told her. He flipped to the next page in his hands. "All right, Andrew. What's your story?"

Andrew launched into his extensive experience at the Olive Garden in Ithaca. Richard nodded, making a couple of notes on his clipboard. Lara tried to keep from staring at Andrew's emerald-green eyes by focusing on an ancient coffee stain on the tabletop.

"I'm sorry to interrupt," the hostess apologized as she approached their booth. "The chicken delivery's here."

"Finally!" Richard stood. "Hang on a minute, guys," he said as he headed for the kitchen.

Lara turned to Andrew and murmured conspiratorially, "I think we've got this in the bag."

Andrew's eyes sparkled with amusement. "Was my expertise on Italian cuisine impressive enough, you think?" The booth's worn cushion squeaked as he twisted around to look into her face.

Lara nodded soberly. "Your campaign to eliminate spaghetti from the menu was awe-inspiring. Noble, even."

He shook his head as if the defeat still pained him. "It's the least interesting pasta. I was trying to get people out of their comfort zones."

"People *like* being comfortable," she pointed out.

"That's because they've never even tried pappardelle with meatballs. Or even gemelli. There's a whole other world of carbs out there."

"Maybe Richard will be more open to your ideas," she offered. "I'll put in a good word for maligned pasta shapes."

Andrew was still smiling at her when Richard returned to the booth. After a few more perfunctory questions, Richard slapped his thick hand on the worn wooden table-top. "Welcome aboard, mates. You'll both start tomorrow, the three to eleven shift."

Relieved to have the job, Lara thanked him and headed outside. It took Andrew about thirty seconds to catch up to her. Which was about twenty seconds longer than she'd hoped.

"Where are you headed?" he asked, falling into stride beside her.

Lara shrugged, glancing down the bustling street. "I have a few minutes to kill, actually."

He scratched the back of his neck and bit the corner of his lower lip. *Swoon.* "Why don't we celebrate our gainful employment? My treat."

"Maybe you should ask for an advance on your three bucks an hour . . . ." Lara followed Andrew as he headed toward the nearby marina dock.

"Are you kidding? Tips, baby! With this face and my undeniable charm, I'll be the Bill Gates of Pebble Beach in less than a week," Andrew declared as he led her down the adjacent pier.

Lara wrinkled her nose. "The biggest nerd?"

With a heavy sigh, Andrew guided her to a lemonade stand set up in front of a small white sailboat. "I'm talking bills, moola, coin, benjamins. Enough to make a dent in the college fund, anyway."

"Very commendable," Lara affirmed. "I'm saving up for a car."

They sat on a wooden bench on the far end of the pier and tapped their plastic cups together.

"To many benjamins," Lara toasted.

It was the first time they'd faced each other for longer than a second, and she took advantage of the unobstructed view. He had a case of hat head, which made his shaggy hair look all the more adorable. And his warm-with-a-hint-of-mischief smile took over his whole face — eyes, forehead, everything. Plus he seemed smart and witty, two critical qualities that, in Lara's experience, were rarely possessed by cute guys. Granted, she'd only had two real boyfriends, but she'd watched her mother cycle through four husbands in seven years. Given her mom's crazy history with men, Lara wasn't exactly a rush-into-things kind of girl.

After taking a drink, Andrew leaned back and stretched out his arms along the bench, briefly brushing the back of her neck. A tingle radiated from the spot where their skin touched. "I haven't been up here in years. It hasn't changed much."

"This is my first time. It's really beautiful." Lara looked out over the ocean, where boats and Jet Skis bobbed picturesquely in the lapping waves. She pulled her camera out of her slouchy bag and focused on a group of seagulls strutting along the pier. Turning back to Andrew, she zoomed in for a close-up.

She snapped the picture, his green eyes smiling as if just for her.

An hour later, he'd told her all about his childhood summers in Pebble Beach, including the time he'd decided to trap a raccoon to keep as a pet. Unsurprisingly, the raccoon hadn't been entirely cooperative.

"Thankfully I'm much older and wiser now," he finished.

"Oh, really? What wisdom have the years bestowed?" she challenged.

"Well, I can now guarantee that the lobster rolls I'm

going to take you for will be the best you've ever had." Andrew offered her a heart-melting grin.

Lara narrowed her blue eyes. "Don't let Richard hear you say that. You're consorting with the enemy."

Andrew lifted an eyebrow. "I thought I was consorting with *you*."

Lara looked down at her frayed cutoffs and already tanned legs. She'd planned to spend her summer working, not falling into a romantic fling. "What does that involve, exactly?" she asked, looking up with one arched eyebrow.

He fixed his eyes on hers, and she noticed a hint of gray in the green. "Getting to know each other. And possibly a mix CD, if you're extremely lucky."

"Ah, but that depends on how good your taste in music is. Poor song choice could ruin everything we have together."

He cocked his head and looked at her appraisingly. "You might just be the perfect girl."

She tried to swallow, but her throat refused to cooperate. Feeling heat rise to her face, she tried to focus on the seagulls squawking overhead and the relaxing lapping of waves under the dock. But as she looked down to collect herself, her glance fell on her oversized men's Timex. She'd bought it at a drugstore for three dollars. According to its digital face, she was fifteen minutes late to meet her mother, who'd be giving her a ride back to the cottages.

"I have to go," she said regretfully. She had never been so sorry to leave a place in her entire life — and she'd done a lot of leaving in her sixteen years.

Andrew ran a hand through his dark floppy waves as Lara reluctantly stood. She was about to leave him with a pithy good-bye, but the words flew out of her mind when he reached out for her hand and pulled himself up.

He stood close to her — closer than she would have predicted when she met him an hour before. As he looked down at her, the space between them suddenly changed, as if the air had gotten thicker. For the first time in years, Lara couldn't think of a single thing to say.

He stepped forward, and her embarrassment and confusion melted away. The world around her — the seagulls, and the kids begging for more taffy — all went fuzzy. It was just the two of them, moving in slow motion. When his hand gently tucked her hair behind her ear, she actually felt her knees wobble. And as his lips gently brushed against hers, she closed her eyes and pulled him in closer.

Her ride home could wait.

3

Greer Hallsey carelessly yanked her Vuitton luggage out of her white Mercedes CLK and closed the trunk with a satisfying *thunk*. She pushed her huge Chanel sunglasses to the top of her head and squinted at the three white houses that would be her home for the next two months. Or however long it took for her parents to resolve their "issues." She sighed dramatically and looked to the blue ocean spreading out behind them like a rumpled silk sheet.

Okay, so it could have been worse.

She picked her way across the gravel driveway, careful not to scuff her new Jimmy Choo kitten heels. They were sold out at Bergdorf's, and it was only thanks to the divine intervention of her personal shopper that they graced her feet now. Greer didn't know if she was supposed to stay in a particular house, nor did she particularly care, so she just headed for the nearest one. Standing in the front foyer, she listened for sounds of activity. Someone was in the kitchen to her left. Greer considered for a moment, then made a right up the stairs. She could deal with the entirely unpleasant family aspect of this place later.

The rooms were on the small side, but there was nothing to be done about that. She chose one at random and shut the door. Her tan from spring break in the Maldives had faded considerably, and as long as her banishment from New York involved a beach, she might as well rectify that. She stripped down, plucked out the first bikini that poked out of her lingerie bag — her white Dior with the glittering charm in the cleavage — and tied it on. She stepped into the bathroom to snatch a towel and caught her reflection in the small mirror. Her long brown hair was still straight and glossy despite the convertible ride — Greer had co-opted her mother's trick of tying a scarf around her head when she drove.

Slipping downstairs quietly, she peered through the sliding doors for a path to the beach.

"Greer? Is that you?"

Resigned, she walked into the gleaming kitchen. Her aunts Trudy and Claire were busily making hamburger patties.

"Hi," Greer said warily. Even though she'd been sent to live with these people for the summer, she barely knew them. Her own family usually vacationed in far more exotic and exclusive places — and they brought personal trainers and chefs along, not distant relatives.

"It's so good to see you, sweetie." Aunt Claire wiped her hands on a towel and hugged her. Greer endured it stiffly, feeling as claustrophobic as hitting the annual Barneys warehouse sale at the lunch-hour rush. The scent of cheap perfume trailed up from her aunt's neck, and Greer discreetly but firmly pulled away before she coughed.

"How was the drive up from New York?" Aunt Claire asked as she went back to the bowl of raw meat.

Greer grimaced. "Long, but it's good to get out of the city."

"I see you're not wasting any time," Aunt Trudy commented, nodding at Greer's bikini.

"I heard so many good things about Pebble Beach, I wanted to see for myself," she half lied, fidgeting restlessly with the Dior charm. In truth, her mom had sent her to stay with *her* cousins for the summer, even though they weren't particularly close.

"They spend the summers in Myrtle Beach," she'd told Greer erroneously, although Greer had quickly figured out what her mom meant.

"Out those doors, down the steps, and through the gate," Aunt Claire directed. "Dinner's in half an hour, but maybe you can go grab Jessi? She's probably swimming."

Jessi, *Claire's daughter*. Greer hadn't seen her second cousin for years. She knew her about half as well as she knew her manicurist. Blonde, kind of a tomboy, a year younger than her — that was about all she remembered. "Thanks," she replied as she stepped outside.

As she slid the door closed, she could see her aunts' heads huddling together. She could only assume they were talking about how Greer's parents had sent her up here while they worked on their marriage. After watching Mom and Dad alternately shout at and ignore each other for months, Greer wasn't very optimistic about the outcome. But she could do without her aunts gossiping about it.

She stood on the deck and took in the view. The ocean was a peculiar blend of navy and dark gray that looked cold even from a distance. She recalled the vivid turquoise blue of the ocean in Nice last summer — water so warm it felt like a bath. She'd loved being surrounded by European accents, especially the French-speaking waiters who called her *mademoiselle* and served her champagne without making her display her fake ID. Even the towel she held now was thin and scratchy compared to the cloud-soft ones they'd stocked at the resort's infinity pool. She gazed bleakly at the rocky beach, feeling a surge of anger at her parents for dumping

her in Maine. Well, at least there had to be boys here —
and with boys came parties and an excuse to avoid any
annoying family.

She had just reached the gate when she saw a girl in a
dripping-wet bikini walking up the path. Greer studied her
as she approached.

"Greer!" Her cousin still sounded like the same little
girl Greer barely remembered.

"Hey, Jessi," she said coolly. With her light blonde
hair and wide green eyes, Jessi was pretty in an innocent-
looking, Taylor Momsen kind of way, but with Jessica Biel's
killer body.

"Oh, it's Jessica now," her cousin corrected, turning
bright red. How *mature*. "Did you just get in? I met the cutest guys today! You, me, and Lara are going to have the best
time this summer!" She prattled on, oblivious to Greer's
look of confusion.

"Who's Lara?" Greer interrupted.

"Oh, she's our new cousin. Her mom just married Uncle
Mike. You were in Italy or something during the wedding?
They'll be here this summer, too. She's awesome."

Greer groaned inwardly. She wasn't really a big fan of
girl talk, or girlfriends in general. "Great."

Aunt Claire waved at them from the deck. "Come up
and get changed for dinner."

Greer sighed. Her mom was so wrapped up in her own

life, and her dad was a workaholic, so she was used to pretty much complete freedom. But she knew better than to be a brat on her first day, so she dutifully followed Jessi into the house. A host of Tuttles had descended on the kitchen and living room, with Uncle Carr manning the big grill on the deck. Greer tried picturing her father, who rarely wore anything but custom-made suits or golf clothes, sporting an apron. Not a chance.

As she headed for the stairs, Aunt Trudy popped out of the kitchen.

"I moved your bags into Jessi and Lara's room, sweetie. It's the first one on the right."

Greer forced herself not to laugh in her aunt's face. The thought of sharing a room with two strange girls was ludicrous.

"Oh, um . . . " Greer put on her best *I-don't-want-to-be-a-bother-but* . . . face. "I guess I had just hoped to have some space this summer. You know, to think? It's been so tense at home lately, I could really use some alone time."

She could see her aunt's heart softening. "It's just going to be such a tight squeeze, but given the circumstances . . . You keep your room for now, and we'll just move a couple of people around."

Greer grinned as she went up the stairs. Some people were just too easy.

After quickly changing into a peach Mayle dress, she returned to the deck for the gourmet dinner of overcooked burgers and supermarket coleslaw. The large, extended Tuttle family — made up of far too many howling children and clucking moms and dads, as far as Greer was concerned — took up nearly all the deck chairs. Greer grabbed a Diet Coke, wishing she could spike it with vodka, and reluctantly took a seat next to Jessi-*ca*. Her cousin was mooning over how much fun Ella and Beth and Kelsi had had during their summers here. Greer sighed.

"Doing any sports next year?" Jessica asked her, clearly trying to make conversation.

Greer laughed, a little more rudely than she meant to. "I'm not really a joiner."

Jessica took a bite of her burger and tried again. "I'm going to a bonfire tonight, if you want to come."

A party? "Who's going?"

"The guys I met today. They're really cute and —"

"Sounds great," Greer interrupted. She'd heard enough. Hot guys usually had hot friends.

Jessica beamed and Greer smiled back. A local boy would be an interesting change. City boys were just as catty as the girls. But Greer's smile faded when Jessica's parents, along with Uncle Mike and a completely unfamiliar woman, sat on the bench opposite her.

"So when do we have to let Rob know about next year?" Uncle Mike asked, putting his arm around the mystery woman, who Greer could only assume was a new addition to the family. "He'll want to list these houses if we decide not to commit."

Greer noticed her cousin's expression darken.

"What are you talking about?" Jessica demanded across the table. "Why wouldn't we come back? The houses are done! It's the Tuttles Do Pebble Beach 2.0."

"Jess! You know I'd love to keep up the tradition," Aunt Claire answered. "But Maine just isn't as convenient as it used to be. With Mike's family in Chicago and us now in Ithaca . . . we're not really a New England family anymore."

This debate meant nothing to Greer. She was one thousand percent sure she'd be spending next summer in Belize.

Suddenly, Greer felt the bench rock unsteadily beneath her.

"Hey." A thin girl with short black hair grinned at her from Jessica's other side. "Save some cow for me!"

"Woo-hoo! We're all here!" Jessica hugged the girl happily. "You guys haven't met yet! Greer, Lara. Lara, Greer."

"Hey," Greer said, appraising her new cousin. Lara was tiny, with a small face dominated by huge blue eyes. With her cropped hair and thrift-shop style, she looked like a hipster elf. "Welcome to our big, happy family." Greer was unable to keep the sarcasm out of her voice.

"I was just telling Greer about the bonfire we're going to tonight," Jessica reported, oblivious to the look that passed between the two girls. "You're in, right?"

"Sure," Lara said agreeably. "I'm up for anything."

"Great!" Jessica clapped her hands eagerly. "This summer's going to be amazing."

This time last year, Greer had known exactly what she had to look forward to when she deplaned from first class: sun, champagne, and golden-skinned Mediterranean boys. But no matter what continent she was on, there was one surefire way to make things interesting. She raised her almost-empty glass.

"Hear, hear," she intoned. "Now let's go find some boys."

4

"Come on, slowpokes," Greer called, waiting impatiently at the end of the path. She wore a floaty top over tiny white shorts that showed almost every inch of her long legs, and sky-high platforms.

Jessica suppressed an envious sigh — even though her friends back home said she had a great body, the only word she had to describe it was "athletic" — which was almost as unsexy-sounding as oatmeal or Handi Wipes. She hoped she looked decent in her striped H&M sundress.

"What's her deal? Is she going to turn into a pumpkin at midnight?" Lara grumbled as she shuffled through the sun-bleached gate. Jessica giggled.

As the girls made their way down the beach, Jessica

imagined her older cousins sharing exactly this moment a few years ago — walking around like they owned Pebble Beach. It was already everything she'd ever imagined.

The girls approached the crowd, which was gathered around a small bonfire. Little flecks of orange light reflected on the ocean's surface. Most of the partyers were standing around talking, plastic cups in hand, though a Lil' Wayne track had inspired some dancing near the fire. Jessica scanned the faces, but didn't see the one she was looking for.

The girls hadn't taken ten more steps before a short, sandy-haired boy boldly walked directly up to Greer. Jessica watched with amusement as Greer waved him away like an annoying gnat. As Jessica followed the crestfallen boy's retreat, she spotted Connor talking to a small group of guys. She waved at him, and he jogged over.

"You made it," he said, smiling. "So my devastating charm didn't scare you away?"

Jessica grinned. "Charm? I don't recall . . ."

He looked wounded. "That hurts. I'll have to get my revenge during our workouts."

Before Jessica could respond, an arm laid across her shoulder. She turned to find Liam's tanned and lightly freckled face inches from her own.

"Looking good, Tuttle," he told her, sending flutters to her stomach. She was glad she'd decided to wear a dress.

Her usual baggy T-shirts and basketball shorts had no place in her summer of *looove.*

"Thanks," she replied shyly, breathing him in. He smelled like shampoo and soap and, if she was not mistaken, a dash of freaking adorable. She caught sight of Lara looking at them and hastily made introductions.

"It's a pleasure to have you in our houses." Connor jokingly kissed Greer's and Lara's hands, while Liam offered to get everyone drinks. Then Connor loped off to chat with some guys.

"Have fun, we'll catch up later." Greer squeezed Jessi's hand.

"Where are you going?" she asked, panicked.

"Giving you some *alone* time," Greer whispered. "I need my own Prince Charming."

Lara agreed. "She's right. We're going to take a tour of the beach."

As the girls turned to leave, Liam returned balancing four cups. Greer and Lara helpfully plucked two out of his hands, thanking him as they slid past into the crowd. The light from the bonfire made everyone's cheeks glow a little red.

"Cousins, eh?" Liam watched the girls go. He and Jessica sat down on a thick log. "How are the houses?"

"Amazing," Jessica gushed over the thumping bass. She pushed her feet into the cool sand, feeling her heart race at

Liam's nearness. "I can't believe those little cottages grew up to be so gorgeous."

Liam laughed and leaned closer so he didn't have to yell. "It took two years and a lot of work. But it's all worth it to make you happy." Jessica noticed a dimple that was half-hidden by the stubble on his cheeks. Was it possible to be any cuter?

"Could you pull an extreme makeover on our house in Ithaca?" she asked. "We could really use a deck the size of a parking lot in our backyard."

"As long as you promise to lie on it in that blue bikini," he teased. Jessica blushed and sipped her beer. *So this is what flirting feels like?* She listened attentively as Liam launched into his upcoming carpentry apprenticeship in the fall.

"What about school?" she asked when he paused to take a drink.

Liam shook his head. "I graduated in May. And I'll learn way more working than I would in college," he replied confidently. "Plus, I'll be making bank while everyone's talking about their feelings in Intro to Philosophy."

She nodded. Liam seemed older than seventeen, even older than her brother Jordan, who was turning nineteen in September. "Makes sense," she said, even though she wasn't sure. School was important to Jessica — it was hard to imagine not going to college.

"I'm a smart guy," he said with a wink. On any other guy, it would've been cheesy, but somehow he managed to look sexy and mischievous. "Besides, it'll leave more time for me to focus on my surfing."

Jessica shifted on the log, her hand brushing against Liam's leg accidentally, though he didn't seem to notice. They talked about surfing and the thrill of competition. She got so engrossed in their conversation that she didn't notice her cousins return.

Lara slid down next to Jessica. "How's it going?" she whispered. Greer stood close by, looking bored.

"Good," Jessica whispered back. "Really good!"

Liam draped an arm comfortably around Jessica's shoulder and she settled against it.

"So, ladies," he drawled in his faint Maine accent. "How was your grand tour?"

"The view could be better," Greer remarked, glancing at a group of boys who were ogling her legs from across the fire.

Liam laughed, and his arm tightened around Jessica's shoulder. She contentedly sipped her beer.

Greer looked down at her empty cup. "I think I need a refill," she announced. "Anyone else?"

Liam swallowed the remainder of his drink. "The hottest girl at the party wants to get me a beer? Can't say no to that." Liam held his empty cup in front of Greer, who hesitated a moment before grabbing it.

Jessica froze. Had she heard him right? His arm was still resting on her shoulder, but unless she was mistaken, he'd just called Greer hot. Did that make her . . . not?

Abruptly, she felt herself being hoisted up. Lara stood next to her.

"It's getting late, we should head home," Lara told Liam with steel in her voice.

"You just got here," he remarked. "What's the rush?"

"Early day tomorrow," Lara snapped, putting a firm arm around Jessica's shoulders. As she was dragged through a throng of dancers, Jessica glanced back, hoping Liam was following her. But he was talking with some guys and didn't turn around.

Confused and hurt, Jessica walked side by side with Lara into the darkness. The laughter and music followed them down the beach, but for Jessica the party was over.

Greer watched as a slightly sunburned brunette slid into Jessica's spot on the driftwood log. She rolled her eyes. She could detect a player from a hundred yards away, and Liam had JERK written all over his deeply tanned forehead. She spun on her heel and walked away, wondering what Jessica could possibly see in this guy.

She paused as she passed the keg. *One for the road?* Why not.

As she expertly tilted her Solo cup to pour the perfect beer, a tall blond boy came up next to her. When nothing but foam spurted into her cup, Greer quickly removed the pump from the top of the empty keg and tapped the one next to it. She topped off her glass, not spilling a drop. The guy let out a long, low whistle as she finished pouring.

Greer was amused in spite of herself. "You've never seen a keg tapped before?"

"Not like that, I haven't." He looked at her with admiration. "You made it into an art form."

"Thanks," Greer said, mollified. She was wearing four-inch platforms, but he still towered over her. His dark blond hair had sun-lightened streaks. A smattering of freckles peppered his nose and his eyes were an incredibly clear blue. She didn't usually go for the all-American look, but there was something open and confident about him. "Is this a ploy to get me to pour one for you?"

He laughed. "I wouldn't turn you down. Where'd you get those kind of skills?"

"Lots and lots of practice." It was true. Greer's father had loved it when she brought him his drink of choice after a late night at the office. Granted, that was a rum and soda, but her alcohol education had been well-rounded at friends' prep-school parties. "My dad appreciated my bartending skills," she clarified.

"I promise to appreciate them, too," he offered.

She considered this for a moment, examining his face in the soft light of the bonfire, then picked up a cup. "No promises on taste. New Yorkers prefer their beer imported."

"City girl, huh?" He raised his eyebrows. A sudden breeze whipped his dirty-blond hair in front of his eyes.

She noted his skepticism. "Bad impression of us?"

"It's getting better," he responded. "I'm Brady, by the way."

"Greer," she replied. "Hand me that cup?" She glanced at him with a smile, just in time to see him frown. She paused.

"Greer?" he repeated slowly. "And you're from New York?"

"Do I know you?" She felt dread rise up in her stomach. This party just refused to be fun.

Brady's smile returned, but with a new smugness. "Nope, but I know *of* you. Noah Michaels is a buddy of mine from Putney."

Noah Michaels. Nice boy, brown eyes, a little vanilla but very sweet. She'd met him at a one of her parents' fundraisers last Christmas. He'd come down from boarding school in Vermont to visit her a few weeks later, and — to his detriment — brought along his rowing-captain roommate, Christian, who had a penchant for clubbing. Needless to say, she'd hooked up with the roommate, Noah found out, and the rest was Greer's history. Whatever.

She turned on her megawatt smile, which generally caused guys to lose their trains of thought. "Noah was great. We just didn't have much in common," she explained. It wasn't a big deal. And it had happened months ago, which might as well be a lifetime as far as she was concerned.

This time, Brady's laugh was devoid of humor. "From

what I remember, you ended up having a lot in common with Christian. I know what girls like you are like, but *man.* . . ." He shook his head ruefully. "Noah was really messed up after that."

"Girls like me?" Greer glared at Brady, angered.

"Yeah, he's with a tennis player now," Brady said with a hint of relief, as if Noah had finally come to his senses. He picked up his drink. "Anyway, it was good meeting you."

"Same," Greer replied stonily, watching him go. She took her drink and wandered around the fire, thinking about Noah's tennis-playing girlfriend. It was weird that Brady had described her that way. How did guys describe *her*? That hottie with the legs? The chick with those insane shoes? That bitchy girl who thinks she's too good for everyone? As she reached the fringes of the crowd, she saw Liam's little brother again and waved him over. She had an idea.

"Hey, Connor. Do you know anything about that guy Brady?"

Connor nodded. "We went to elementary school together, but he goes to boarding school now. His parents own the yacht club."

Greer smiled sweetly. "Keep going."

"He gives sailing lessons," Connor continued. "Oh, and he broke up with his girlfriend, Kaitlyn, a few weeks ago. They've been dating since, like, kindergarten," he said, shaking his head in wonder. "I heard she cheated on him, so he's sworn off girls for like a year or something."

"Thanks, Connor. I owe you one."

"Sure. Uh, where's Jessica?"

Jessica? Greer looked at Connor quizzically before she realized who he was talking about. "She left with Lara." She handed him her empty cup, turned, and kept walking, ignoring a chorus of "hey, beautiful"s as she went.

Greer kicked off her platforms and strolled barefoot in the cold sand, heading back toward the house. She needed a project to keep her busy, and Brady fit the bill nicely. He was cute, funny, and sailed yachts — perfect summer romance material. The fact that he had already quasi-rejected her — *and* was recovering from a breakup — made the challenge all the more appealing. She lived for challenges. Particularly when they were over six feet tall.

Greer quickened her pace toward home. Tomorrow was going to be an early morning. She had a sudden desire to sign up for sailing lessons. . . .

Lara walked Jessica to the back deck of their house, sitting her down in a lounge chair. Despite Lara's best efforts, Jessica hadn't said a word since they left the party. Lara's maternal instincts, which were already well-honed thanks to her mother's flightiness, kicked in.

"Hey," Lara began, unfolding a blanket from the end of the chaise. She wrapped it around them both. "Let's talk about it, okay?"

Jessica didn't acknowledge her. Lara was beginning to get concerned, when she saw a small smile play along her cousin's lips.

"Do you think Greer would let me borrow those shorts for the next party?"

Lara stared at her for a second before cracking up. After a moment, Jessica joined her. "I was worried about you," Lara said. "He's just a guy, you know. There are plenty of others, even in this tiny town."

Jessica's laughter faded. "I know, but he's so . . ." she trailed off.

"You've only known him for one day," Lara reasoned. "But, if you're really into him, give it a little time. He was probably drunk."

"Drunk on Greer's perfect legs," Jessica said glumly. "I can't compete with that."

Lara giggled. "You've got pretty hot legs yourself, babe. And besides, I doubt Greer is interested in him."

Jessica sighed. "But is *he* interested in her?"

Lara stared out beyond the deck, hearing the ocean but not seeing it in the inky darkness. She listened to the cicada symphony, musing about her own boy situation. She hadn't mentioned her kiss with Andrew to Jessica or Greer — it still felt too surreal to blab about just yet. But for the first time ever, she couldn't wait to go to work. *Three o'clock tomorrow.*

"Hey, how about giving me that bodyboarding lesson you promised?" Lara asked Jessica, changing the subject. Considering her mother's previous track record in marriages, she should probably enjoy Pebble Beach while she still had the chance. By next summer her mom could be on

40

to husband number six, and she could be stuck in Houston or Timbuktu for the summer. "I have time tomorrow before I start work."

Jessica pulled the blanket up to her chin. "Work?" she asked, her forehead creasing.

"It's a thing people do for money sometimes," Lara deadpanned. "I got a job at Ahoy Grill. It's just a matter of time before I'm menacing the highways in my new car."

"I'll have to come by," Jessica told her, before warning Lara what kind of suit to wear in the morning. "It's a long walk back here when you're buck naked."

"Nobody better be buck naked up there!" a male voice called from the darkness, and the sound of a guy's sandals suddenly clomped up the wooden steps to the deck.

The girls watched as a dark shape rose up the stairs and materialized into a dark-haired teenage boy. Lara's mouth dropped open in astonishment when she recognized Andrew, straight out of her thoughts.

But before Lara could open her mouth, Jessica jumped up and ran over to Andrew, throwing her arms around him.

"You made it!" she cried.

Lara froze, the smile disappearing from her face. *What the hell?*

Jessica dragged Andrew over to a still-speechless Lara. "This is my brother, Drew."

41

Lara's heart halted momentarily, then resumed beating at ten times its normal rate. She tried to speak up, but her throat would only produce a muted gurgle of horror.

Oblivious, Jessica plowed on. "Drew, this is Lara, she's our new cousin — Uncle Mike's stepdaughter. Remember? I went to the wedding?"

Oh. My. God. *OhmygodohmygodohmyGOD!*

Andrew — Drew, apparently — finally noticed Lara in the shadows and stopped short. Under other circumstances, the shocked look on his face would have been hilarious. Right now, not so much.

"Uh, hey," he managed.

"Hey, yourself," Lara said, managing to find her voice at last. "Small world."

Jessica looked back and forth between them. "You know each other?"

Lara and Drew exchanged a glance before Lara spoke up. "We both got jobs at Ahoy today." That sounded innocent enough, and she wasn't about to volunteer that the interview was followed by a semi-date and the best kiss she'd ever had.

"And you had no idea you were cousins!" Jessica laughed gleefully. "That's hilarious!"

Lara and Drew flinched. *Cousins.* The significance was beginning to dawn on both of them.

Drew shifted awkwardly from side to side. "Uh, I'm pretty beat, I think I'll hit the sack." He barely finished his sentence before escaping into the house next door to where the girls were staying.

"Good night!" Jessica called through the sliding glass door. "That was weird," she observed, sitting back down next to Lara. "He's usually much friendlier."

"How — uh, how long has he been your brother?" Lara stuttered. She couldn't think straight. She'd made out with her new cousin. *If Mom's marriage addiction doesn't send me to therapy, this definitely will.* Jessica was staring at her. "I mean, I forgot you had a brother."

"Yeah, two. Jordan's working at a camp a few towns over. Drew had to take him some stuff today, that's why he missed dinner."

Note to self: Do not hook up with any camp counselors. Ever.

"Drew's saving up for college." Jessica went on relentlessly. "He's applying to Cornell, where Jordan goes, so they'll both be close to home," she added proudly.

Lara was only half listening. She felt a profound sadness as this new revelation sunk in. Did he really have to be her *cousin?* It was like a cosmic joke, except the punch line was more like a sucker punch. How could she work next to him after this? How was she going to live so close to him for the *whole summer*? "Oh, God," she moaned, dropping her head into her hands.

Jessica shot her a look of concern. "What's wrong?"

Lara lifted her head and looked at her. She opted for the answer that was less traumatic for both of them.

"I'm getting hungover," Lara lied.

Jessica eyed her skeptically. "Who gets a hangover when they're still drunk?"

"I do," Lara said, standing up. "I'm going to sleep. Will you be okay?"

Jessica nodded. "I'll be in later." Lara had forgotten they were sharing a room. "Are you still up for bodyboarding in the morning?"

Lara closed her eyes. She couldn't bear the thought of making small talk with Drew over Cheerios while rocking pajamas and crusty eye boogers. "Absolutely," she answered with a sigh. "I wouldn't miss it."

7

"The thing with bodyboarding is that you sort of have to get wet," Jessica explained patiently.

Lara danced back from the water in her black '50s-style one-piece suit as another cool gust of wind whipped across the beach. "Hey, I didn't sign up for the Polar Bear Club. Have some mercy."

Jessica hid a smile. She was secretly relieved that Greer had just rolled over when they tried to wake her for this lesson. She couldn't have handled both of them complaining. After a good night's rest, she was feeling much better, but Liam still weighed on her mind.

"This was your idea, so quit whining. Just jump in. It's like ripping off a Band-Aid."

"And I thought you were sweet when we met," Lara grumbled.

"My lacrosse coach would've thrown you in headfirst by now," Jessica informed her cousin, and then, without warning, Lara ran past her toward the water, smacking Jessica's butt loudly along the way.

Grinning, Jessica followed her into the shallow water with the two boards they'd found in the garage. They strapped on their fins and leashes in the bitingly cold water as Jessica went through the basics. Lara listened attentively as Jessica cautioned her about the strong rip currents.

"Got it. Let's go!"

"Let's just paddle out and watch the waves. If they're too high, we'll have to scrap it."

Obligingly, Lara lay on the short board and flailed her arms and legs wildly, only occasionally hitting the water. Jessica hung back, trying not to laugh at her cousin's pathetic-but-entertaining lack of coordination. Eventually, Lara got the hang of it and triumphantly propelled herself farther into the ocean.

"Come back," Jessica called. "The waves are coming in."

Lara stuck her tongue out and kept going. The approaching wave wasn't huge, but big enough to teach Lara a sweet lesson. Jessica caught a glimpse of Lara's comical "oh, crap" expression before she was tumbled into the churning water.

Hooting with laughter, Jessica paddled over as a sodden Lara dragged herself back onto the board and aimed for shore.

"So, as I was saying," Jessica continued as if there had been no interruption, "we should watch to see where the waves break. It'll show us the general area where we can catch the next one."

Still sputtering, Lara flashed her a sour look. Jessica kept pace as Lara crawled onto the beach, dragging her bodyboard behind her like it was a flat dog. Collapsing on her back, Lara gazed up at Jessica. "You're fired."

"You look like you could use a breakfast sundae," Jessica extended a hand to pull Lara up. The two girls carried their fins and boards up the beach to the Okay Café, a gaily painted, '50s-style scoop shop. They dumped their stuff beside a wooden outdoor table as an overly pierced girl sauntered up to take their order.

"Two banana splits," Jessica told her. The waitress nodded and left.

Lara shook off the excess water from her already drying short hair. "Isn't it early for ice cream?"

"Bananas are a breakfast food." Jessica scanned the beach, shading her eyes against the high sun.

"When you put it that way . . ." Lara glanced at her digital watch. "I don't have to be at work till three, so I might have time for a Caramel Turtle for lunch."

Jessica frowned. Her idea of a perfect summer included a lot of cousinly hang-out time, but Lara had committed most of her days to Ahoy. So much for spontaneous adventures and nonstop bonding. And Greer didn't seem too friendly. Which made the other criteria for a perfect summer even more important.

"Actually, I wanted to ask your advice," Jessica began hesitantly. Not even the morning's aquatic comedy had been able to get her thoughts away from her boy dilemma. "It's about last night."

She saw Lara stiffen. "Don't worry," Jessica added quickly. "I'm not upset anymore, I just need a strategy."

"A strategy for what?" Lara asked, shoving a spoonful of chocolate ice cream into her mouth.

"Do you think I need to be more — you know," Jessica searched for the right words. "Noticeable? To guys?" she finished lamely. "I mean, you're the funny one with the great style. And Greer's the rich, gorgeous destroyer of guys' souls. So what's my thing?"

"I don't know what you mean," Lara said gently. "Your 'thing'?"

Jessica ran her hand across the smooth surface of the Formica tabletop. "I've just been wondering what guys think of me," she admitted.

She'd always had lots of guy friends, and she grew up with two older brothers. Hanging out with boys had never been a big deal. But seeing Greer and Lara at last night's party, totally self-assured, made Jessica feel a little immature and silly. With four stepfathers, Lara had obviously been through a lot. And Greer's experience as a city girl practically oozed out of her invisible pores. So far, the biggest drama in Jessica's life had been a stress fracture during last year's basketball season.

Lara took a deep breath. "I know we haven't really known each other all that long, but I've got a pretty good idea about the kind of person you are. You're smart and funny, you're genuine, and you're amazing at sports. Not to mention, you're beautiful. Guys notice you, for real."

Jessica blushed. "But if all that's true, then what did I do wrong?"

"You didn't do anything wrong. At all. Maybe the problem is Liam. I mean, what do you actually know about him?

"He's hot," Jessica acknowledged.

"Hopefully there's a little something underneath," Lara commented drily. "I generally like guys I have something in common with — musical taste, sense of humor, that kind of thing. The next time you see him, try and talk about something he's into."

Jessica sighed. *That* was the problem. When she was around Liam, she hardly even remembered what she was into, let alone how to make conversation about what *he* liked. "How am I supposed to do that? My brain is Jell-O around him." She bopped her head from side to side. "Jiggle jiggle."

Laughing, Lara dropped her spoon into the empty sundae dish with a clang. "Like I said, you're smart. Do a little detective work."

Jessica considered the soupy remains of her own sundae. The first thing that came to her mind was stalking, but that seemed too time-consuming. She had boogie boarding to do, and a tan to work on, let alone her lax training. She was actually supposed to start her training regimen today. *Wait. . . .*

"Perfect!" Jessica cried, startling her cousin. The elderly couple at the table nearest them turned to stare. Oops. "*Connor*," she told Lara quietly. "We're supposed to train for lacrosse together. I can totally dig for info about Liam while we practice."

Lara squinted at her. "Just try not to make it so obvious."

"Right," Jessica agreed, suddenly feeling energized. "Let's go wake up Greer! Maybe she'll give me some tips!"

Lara looked hesitant, but gave Jessica a thumbs-up. "Why not? Knowing how to destroy a boy's soul might come in handy."

Greer slouched in her car, fidgeting with the laces on her leather-wrapped steering wheel. Through her iPhone's speaker, her mother's voice gushed about her recent election to chair the Frick Collection Charity Ball. Greer grunted now and then, not really listening. She was staring at the squat white building in front of her, displaying a navy sign with STEWART YACHT CLUB tastefully lettered in gold. She'd made the mistake of returning her mother's voice mail from the previous night on the drive over, and consequently had been stuck in the parking lot for the past fifteen minutes.

"Anyway, darling, was there anything in particular you needed? You know I have my touch-up in half an hour."

Greer rolled her eyes. Since the dawn of time, her mother had had a standing appointment at Frédéric Fekkai every other morning for a blowout, with a mani/pedi once a week. Except for vacations, she'd only missed her "touch-up" once — when she was giving birth to Greer. Her mother liked to tell the story with a fake-embarrassed laugh, followed by a whispered admission that she'd arranged to have her hairstylist driven to the hospital later that day. As a result of this diligence, not a single photo existed of Cassandra Hallsey looking anything but perfectly polished, even after twelve hours of labor.

"Hello? Are you there?" Her mother's impatient voice cut through Greer's thoughts.

"I'm here. And I was just returning your call. How are you and Daddy doing?"

"Oh." Cassandra's voice was even more clipped than usual. "I'm fine, dear. Your father has been staying at a loft in Tribeca," her mother informed her. "You can reach him there if you want to. Now I've really got to go. Kisses!"

"Bye," Greer said, but her iPhone indicated that the call had already ended. She debated calling her dad at the office, but she knew that the chances of him picking up were slim. His assistant always said he was in meetings, which Greer figured was usually true. As a managing director of a hedge fund, his life seemed like one long boring meeting, occasionally interrupted by a fight with her mother or an affair with someone barely older than Greer herself.

She tossed the phone into her plum Chloé bag and

finally got out of the car, smoothing down her seersucker miniskirt. Paired with a baby blue Lacoste polo, the outfit said *pretty*, *sweet*, and *take-me-home to mom*. Perfect for Brady. Greer stepped into the office and spotted a girl, twelve-ish, with Brady's blond hair and blue eyes standing behind the desk. *Younger sister*, Greer concluded.

"Can I help you?" the girl asked with a friendly smile. Her name tag had a sailboat on it and read CLARA.

"Hi, Clara. I'd like to take sailing lessons." Greer couldn't help smiling back.

"Great! What's your experience level?"

Greer thought for a second. She'd been on plenty of boats in her life, but she never paid attention to how they actually *worked*. "None."

"Okay." Clara handed her a clipboard and a blue pen with the club's logo on it. "Fill out these forms and look over the price list. Did you want to start today?"

"Yes!" Greer responded, a little too enthusiastically. "Preferably with Brady."

"I'll check his schedule. BRB!"

Greer shook her head. She'd never wanted a younger sister, but it might be nice having someone who said BRB on some of life's suckier days. Like when you find out your parents have separated. Or two weeks before finals, when you accidentally discover your father's affair with his intern. She quickly filled in the forms, opting for two private lessons per week, the most frequent beginner plan offered. Clara returned, trailed by a middle-aged couple wearing matching Stewart Yacht Club polo shirts. Greer plastered on her especially-for-parents smile and stood up.

"Here you go, Clara," she said sweetly, handing over the clipboard. Greer stepped forward and held out her hand. "I'm Greer Hallsey. Pleasure to meet you."

The woman shook it warmly. She was several inches shorter than Greer, but trim and pretty. "I'm Ellen and this is Gerald. And I see you've met our daughter. Welcome to the club!"

"We'll make a sailor out of you before you know it!" Gerald's years on the water showed on his ruddy, weathered face.

"Thank you," she replied graciously. "I'm looking forward to that."

Clara stood by her parents, and the three of them beamed at her. Brady's parents were so . . . *nice*. His whole family was. It was a little disconcerting, actually. As if someone was going to pop out now and say to her, "See? *This* is what a family is supposed to be like."

"Well, let's get you started!" Gerald boomed. His belly strained against the fabric of the polo. "We have a safety video for you to watch, then we'll get you out on the water."

Greer followed Brady's dad into a small classroom and waited as he fumbled with the DVD player. She wondered how Brady would react when he saw her. She knew he wasn't the type to fall for the standard sex-kitten act, but that's what made this fun. If only he would show up.

After the DVD got going, Greer settled into a chair and watched as a sailor strapped a life vest onto a child. *Boring*.

"Funny seeing you here," a familiar voice said just as the credits began to roll. Greer kept her eyes trained on the video for a moment longer, trying to appear as fascinated as possible, then turned around.

Brady stood just inside the doorway, looking whole-some in his white Stewart Yacht Club polo shirt and khaki cargo shorts. He was holding her clipboard.

"Hey." Greer smiled, holding her hands primly in her seersucker lap. "I wish I could say it was a coincidence, but I'm not a liar."

"Oh?" he inquired, one eyebrow raised.

Ouch.

"Connor mentioned that you gave sailing lessons. I thought it sounded fun, so here I am."

Brady consulted the clipboard. "Well, at two lessons a week, you'll be having a lot of fun," he noted, his blond eye-brows knit together. "Look, we're pretty busy around here during the season, so I hope you're serious about learn-ing. Otherwise . . ."

Okay, so she hadn't expected him to warm up to her immediately, but did he have to be so uninterested?

"Look, I know what you think of me, but there's not much I can do about that." She shrugged carelessly. "If you want me to go with another instructor, I'd appreciate a recommendation." Greer held her breath, waiting.

She crossed her long tan legs and caught him glancing at them. There, that was more like it.

"No, that's okay." *Exhale.* "I just wanted to make sure this wasn't some sort of game."

She appreciated his candor, even if he was right on the mark. "No games," she lied. "But I'm finished with the video."

"Then let's get started."

Brady and his dad hoisted the sail on a small boat, while his mother stood on the dock next to Greer, maintaining friendly chatter.

"He's been out on the water since he was born. We taught him to swim before he could walk!" The pride in her voice was unmistakable.

"Mom, what lies are you spreading about me now?" Brady vaulted off the boat onto the dock beside them. He put his arm around his mother's shoulders and squeezed affectionately. Greer felt a pang of envy — she couldn't remember ever acting so comfortable around her own family. Even when she was a little girl, she remembered feeling stiff and out of place with her parents.

His mother held a hand up with mock gravity. "Nothing but the truth, so help me God." She turned to Greer. "Looks like you're all set. Have fun."

"Brady'll take good care of you," Gerald rumbled as he climbed off the boat. "We'll see you in an hour."

Brady held out a hand and helped her onto the boat, admiring her white-soled shoes. "Pretty fancy," he commented with a laugh.

"I had them around," she replied airily. Greer was always prepared for a fashion challenge, and last season's light-soled Lanvin flats did the trick.

He finished doing the rigging and tugged at the lines.

Greer jumped up. "I'll check the wind." She knew that Brady was still suspicious of her motives. And she did actually *want* to learn how to sail. Especially if that meant she sailed right into his heart. She could picture drifting on the deck of a sixty-foot yacht in the Aegean Sea, Brady keeping her warm and safe and —

"Hey, can you grab this?" He tossed a heavy rope at her. "Tie it to the jib."

She did as she was told and, working together, they quickly had the small boat gliding across the inlet. "You can relax now," Brady told her.

Greer sat in the cockpit, pleased that she'd done

everything right. Sailing was turning out to be more interesting than she thought. "How long have you been doing this?" she asked conversationally.

Brady adjusted the tiller. "My parents built the club when I was four," he answered. "I can't really remember a time when boats haven't been part of my life."

"That sounds like a pretty idyllic way to grow up," Greer commented. "Your parents are really nice. Clara, too." She wasn't even kissing ass. She really meant it.

"Yeah, they're cool," Brady acknowledged, running his hand along the glossy wooden steering wheel. "What about you?"

Greer fought the urge to laugh. Her parents weren't big believers in quality time. She'd had nannies until she started high school. Her father worked nonstop and her mother was preoccupied by her various charities. She couldn't remember the last time they had a meal together. The Stewarts probably ate dinner together every night. She pictured lots of talking and laughing. It was a totally alien concept.

"They're great," she lied smoothly. "They're renovating the apartment this summer, so I came up here." She had no idea why she lied. No, actually, she did. Explaining her parents' current relationship to Brady would be like describing the difference between Barneys and Bergdorf's —

completely outside his frame of reference. With a family like his, he just wouldn't get it.

He smiled for the first time since the lesson began. "That's cool." He steered the boat along the forested edge of the water. "This is my favorite place." Brady slowed the boat so that it rocked serenely in the lapping blue water.

Greer stood up and looked around. They'd reached another inlet, much smaller than the one where the yacht club was located. This one was forested on two sides, with a long, grassy meadow stretching out on the third. It was undeniably romantic.

"Oh, look!" she whispered excitedly, grabbing on to his sleeve. She pointed at a dark shape in the middle of the field. "I think that's a moose!" Greer wasn't exactly the crunchy nature type — no hiking boots in her shoe closet — but the idea of seeing an animal out in the wild was very cool.

Brady squinted, shielding his eyes from the sun. His face broke into a broad grin. "I think you're right."

They watched the moose silently as it ambled around the meadow to graze, its wide antlers impressive even from the far distance. Greer wasn't sure how much time had passed when she turned to ask Brady a question and caught him staring at her. Greer smiled and turned back to the moose. She was a little surprised at how gratified she felt.

It'd been a while since she had innocent fun with a guy, and this wasn't even a date.

"Let's head back," Brady said, clearing his throat and trimming the sail to catch the light wind. "Ready to tack?"

"Aye, captain." She hurried to the pulleys and diligently repeated the tacking procedure that Brady had taught her.

"Nice job, sailor." Brady looked legitimately impressed. "You're a good student."

"Thanks," Greer replied, pulling her wind-whipped dark hair into a messy ponytail. The warmth of the sun on her face felt fantastic, and the carefree feeling of the wide-open ocean was intoxicating. "Where's my gold star?"

Brady laughed. "You can get one from Clara. I ran out this morning."

"So have I graduated to steering yet?" Greer asked eagerly.

"You've still got a ways to go," he replied, smiling. "Maybe in a few weeks."

"You'd be surprised," she told him archly. "I'm a fast learner."

"I have no doubt."

As the boat flew through the water, Greer basked in the sunshine and felt victorious. Brady was already warming up, and she had a guaranteed hour alone with him twice a week for the rest of the summer.

This was going to be almost too easy.

Carrying her Converse low-tops in one hand and her vintage beaded purse in the other, Lara tiptoed out the front door of the house and started down Peachtree Road.

She'd managed to avoid bumping into Drew since last night, which was a miracle with the whole family rambling around all three houses all day. But she knew her luck was about to end. As she turned down Shore Boulevard, she thought about what to say and how to act, but hadn't come up with any good ideas by the time she pulled open Ahoy's glass door.

Drew was already there, talking to Richard and the redheaded hostess. The hostess was smiling up at Drew, causing an unfamiliar knot to tighten in Lara's stomach.

At the sound of the door, everyone turned and Lara

immediately spotted the determination behind Drew's tight smile.

Here goes.

"Right, here's Lara," Richard said by way of greeting, running his hand through his close-cropped blond hair. "I'll give you the grand tour. There's side work to be done when you aren't waiting on customers."

Carefully avoiding eye contact, Drew and Lara followed Richard through the swinging kitchen doors. A few cooks in white chef smocks and checkered pants nodded to them as they were introduced. Back in the dining area, Richard showed them how to refill the salad bar and beverage station. Lara found it nearly impossible to pay attention with Drew at her side. Drew seemed to be making a concerted effort to ignore her as well.

After learning the basic rules ("Don't drop anything and see to the customers"), Lara and Drew tied on their serving aprons and hit the floor. The hostess showed them their stations, and Lara couldn't help noticing that she gave Drew the tables nearest to her stand. Since the dinner rush was still about an hour out, Drew and Lara set to cutting vegetables to restock the salad bar.

Standing side by side, Lara picked up a knife and sliced the top off a bell pepper. Her fingers were trembling a little. She knew she should say something — it seemed ridiculous that they couldn't talk after all the making out they did yesterday.

"So, should I call you Andrew, Drew, or just Cuz?" She broke the ice.

Drew gave her a sideways look and broke into an impossibly cute smile. Life was so unfair.

"Drew's good," he said, switching his focus back to the cucumber he was slicing. "Um, we should probably talk about yesterday. . . ."

"Probably," Lara agreed. "Think we broke any laws?"

He hacked into a head of cabbage and then looked at her. "With our luck."

"Let's just forget about it," she suggested with a cheerfulness she didn't remotely feel. "It's not a big deal."

Drew's thick brows furrowed momentarily. "I guess that's right," he said slowly. He gave her a searching look, then smiled again. "It's too bad. I was really looking forward to . . ." He trailed off.

"I know. Me, too." Lara was quiet, then groaned. "It's like an episode of *True Life*: 'Accidental Incest.'"

"So, friends?" he asked, looking straight at her.

"Friends," Lara agreed, setting her knife down. Was there any other choice?

"Looks like the dinner crowd is coming in." Drew wiped his hands off on a towel. "Wish me luck."

"Break a leg," Lara replied, watching his tall, slender frame head toward a table of giggling surfer girls.

With a sigh, Lara dumped her sliced red pepper into a tub and wiped down the salad area.

"Hey," a female voice spoke up behind her. Lara turned to see a girl with long dark hair and a tiny glittering nose ring. The first word that came to mind was *exotic*. The girl had the most amazing skin color, like a jar of honey with the sun shining through it.

"I'm Zoe, one of the other waitresses."

"I'm Lara," she responded. "I'm new, so I'm sorry in advance for screwing up."

Zoe chuckled and wound her hair into a knot on top of her head, securing it with a pencil. An assortment of gold bangles tinkled as she moved her arms. "No worries. Richard runs a crazy ship, but we get by. Where are you from?"

"Outside Chicago." It seemed like ages since she'd begun the long drive to Pebble Beach with her mom and stepfather number five. "I'm just here for the summer." She was grateful for the distraction of another person besides off-limits Drew and the less-than-friendly hostess.

Just then, a crowd of sixteen people arrived. The hostess seated them in Lara's station and flashed her a smug smile. It was a birthday dinner, and they'd evidently pregamed somewhere else. Lara turned to Zoe with a look of panic.

"All right then, let's feed these bastards," Zoe announced companionably. "I've got your back."

With Drew pitching in as well, Lara managed to take orders and serve the partyers without any problems. Happy and full, they laughed and belched their way out of the restaurant, leaving Lara a generous tip that she unsuccessfully tried to share.

"Believe me, it all evens out in the end," Zoe assured her as Lara thanked her for the millionth time. There was a lull in new customers, and no one seemed to need a water refill just yet. "So what's going on with you and Drew?" she added casually.

"What do you mean?" Lara asked stiffly. She'd been following a strict nonflirting code of behavior.

Zoe grinned wickedly. "Who're you kidding? He's been staring at you all day."

"Um, I didn't notice," she said, even though she'd been aware of his moves around the dining room, the way he laughed at Richard's occasional attempts at brusque humor and remembered to mix half Diet and half regular Cokes for a remarkably whiny couple in the corner.

"Seriously? Because I'm pretty sure you were checking him out, too," Zoe crowed triumphantly. "Not that I can blame you. The boy's adorable."

Lara flushed. Okay, maybe they'd brushed together a few more times than necessary. Still, she had to set the record straight. She didn't think she could take a whole summer of Zoe's too-accurate insinuations.

"Gross. He's my cousin!"

That should shut her up.

As predicted, Zoe did a double take. "Cousins? Oh, man." She didn't seem to know what else to say. Lara almost delighted at her confusion.

Drew came up and swatted Lara with his dish towel. "Still standing?"

Lara smiled weakly. "Thanks for your help, seriously. There's no way I could have done it all on my own."

Drew mimicked the woman whose requests took up a whole page in Lara's notepad. "I want the house salad, with no red onions, no mushrooms, no garlic, no cheese, no cabbage, no tomatoes, and no nuts. And absolutely, positively, no dressing of any kind."

"What was in her salad then? Air?" Zoe settled into an empty booth next to them.

Lara giggled. "Just iceberg lettuce and carrots."

"I'd be cranky, too, if that's all I ate!" Zoe snickered. She noticed one of her tables gesturing at her. "Oops, see ya," she said, standing up.

Alone, Lara and Drew regarded each other, and the air crackled with electricity. Thankfully, a slew of customers poured in, and they had to get up and work.

The rest of the shift went quickly. Lara kept her conversations with Drew strictly platonic, and they got along so well that Lara could almost envision being just friends. *Almost.*

When her shift ended at eleven o'clock, Lara untied her apron with relief. The jukebox had been turned up and people were dancing with beer bottles in hand. Zoe wasn't done for another hour, so Lara found herself standing outside with Drew at 11:05. He offered her a ride home again, and this time she accepted. As he swung the car out of the lot, Lara settled comfortably into her seat.

"You smell like marinara sauce," she commented, wrinkling her nose.

"And you smell like crabs. I mean, *crab*," he returned with an evil smile. She punched him on the shoulder as he pulled out of the parking lot. "Hey! No hitting the driver," he added in a mock-serious tone.

"Do your feet hurt?" she asked as they cruised down the sandy one-lane street. "Mine are killing me."

He glanced over at her in sympathy. "We'll get used to it in a few days," he assured her. "When's your next shift?"

"I think we're both working again tomorrow," Lara replied absently, then cringed in the darkness. She hadn't meant to reveal that she'd looked at his schedule. Memorized it, actually.

Drew smiled and rolled down his window. Cool, salty air whipped through the car. "Should be fun. How'd you make out?"

Lara dug the wad of mostly singles out of her bag and flashed it at him. "Got me a whole mess of washingtons!"

"Hey, sugar mama!" he congratulated her, pulling the car into the crushed granite driveway. He turned off the engine and they sat in the car for a few silent, excruciating seconds while Lara's thoughts flew in different directions: She longed for him to lean over and kiss her and hoped he wouldn't at the same time.

Finally, after what felt like ten lifetimes, Drew pulled open the door handle and got out. Lara sat for a moment, relief and disappointment washing over her, and was surprised when her door popped open and he extended a hand. *Great, he's a frickin' gentleman, too.* There was a tiny static shock when she placed her hand in his palm to get out.

They stood in the driveway, her house's floodlight glaring harshly in their eyes.

"Um, good night," she said quietly, the crickets singing in the background.

"Good night, Lara."

And he was gone.

Jessica knocked on Greer's door, shifting her weight anxiously as she listened for signs of life.

"Umph."

Jessica took that as permission to enter. Greer was spread out luxuriously on her rumpled duvet, eyes closed. Curiously, Jessica sat down on the bed and ran her hand over the supersoft, dove-gray sheets.

"Did you bring these from home?" It would never have occurred to Jessica to bring her own bedding. Though it also wouldn't have occurred to her to sleep till eleven.

Greer opened one eye and peered at her. "They're Frette. I'm used to them," she explained with a yawn.

Jessica sensed her window closing, so she jumped in. "Want to come to town with me?"

Now the other eye was open. "Right now?"

"If you're not too busy," Jessica answered drily, scanning the room. Expensive-looking clothes hung off chairs and sat in haphazard piles on every available surface. Greer was so lucky her parents weren't here. Then again, she was lucky, period.

Greer sighed and sat up. In her white camisole and bedroom hair, she looked like a Victoria's Secret ad. "Does this trip have a purpose?"

Jessica flushed. "I want to look for Connor. We were supposed to train together yesterday, but he had to help his dad do something. I need to make sure we're still on for today."

Greer broke into a sly smile. "You like Connor."

"Er, no." This was actually the third time Jessica had tried going to Greer for advice since yesterday, but her glamorous cousin was never in her room or was out on the beach, surrounded by guys trying to get her attention. Jessica picked up a pillow with a subtle diamond pattern on it. "I want to ask him about Liam."

"Ugh," Greer groaned, throwing her long tan arms over her face. "Are you kidding? He's so . . ."

"So, what?" Jessica asked. "He was really nice when we met."

"There are a million better guys out there," Greer said dismissively. "Why waste your time?"

Easy for Greer to say. With her Angelina Jolie–like looks and her killer body, she was easily the prettiest girl Jessica had ever seen in person. What did she know about finding the right guy, when *every* guy always fell at her feet? "You know what?" Jessica stood up, still holding the pillow. "Never mind. Forget I said anything."

"Suit yourself." Greer grabbed the pillow and put it over her head. "Close the door on your way out," she added with a muffled voice.

Annoyed and hurt, Jessica left Greer's room and wandered downstairs. She wasn't expecting her and Greer to be BFF, but at the very least she'd been hoping for some boy wisdom. As she entered the kitchen, she felt a jolt of surprise.

Connor was on the deck, sitting patiently with a scarred lacrosse stick at his side. He looked up and grinned when she slid open the door.

"Sorry about yesterday. Thought we could get in an extra hour today to make up for it."

"That's okay," Jessica said, her frustration melting away. "Meet me in the yard." Excitedly, she ran out to the garage to snatch her crosse and a few balls, then circled around the house to the backyard.

"Hey," she said breathlessly.

"Good, you're winded," he kidded. "Let's start."

They separated and started passing the ball back and forth. They were at similar skill levels and gradually increased the distance between themselves. It felt good to have the stick in her hands again, and she put Liam out of her head for the time being. She felt the adrenaline start pumping through her veins as Connor began varying his aim, forcing her to sprint to reach the ball in time. She responded by lobbing it far above his head, giggling as she watched him jump frantically to make the catch.

"All right, that's it," Connor growled in mock anger, slamming his stick on the ground. Behind him, a pelican swooped toward the ocean, searching for fish. "You and me. Deathmatch. One for one. First person to miss three loses."

"Done," Jessica said coolly. She was used to guys trying to prove themselves and had a history of making crazy bets with her brothers. "Stakes?"

"Loser goes skinny-dipping." He looked pleased with his idea. "In the middle of the afternoon," he added.

Jessica hesitated. "Clothes off *in* the water, not before."

He considered. "Fine, but you have to wave them over your head for ten seconds."

"Deal." She shook his hand. "Get ready for a really *even* tan."

Over the next half hour, Jessica took her game to another level. Connor was merciless in his passes, pushing the edges of the boundaries they marked off. She kept her focus and went for every pass, determined not to lose. There was *no way* she was going to strip down in broad daylight, with the lifeguards and possibly her family watching. With that in mind, she returned each pass with extra ferocity, jumping for joy when Connor missed it. Connor got even by quickly shooting the ball at the farthest corner of their "field" before she was ready.

"Cheap shot!" Jessica shouted, outraged.

Cackling with triumph, Connor did an idiotic victory dance as she dejectedly retrieved the ball. They were even now, with two misses each. They squared off, staring each other down. Jessica whipped the ball to Connor's left, which smacked easily into his pocket. He smirked and launched the ball way over to her right again, and Jessica ran for her life to catch it. She decided to change up her strategy and aimed the ball extra low. Startled, he dove for it with his crosse outstretched, missing completely and landing heavily on his chest.

"Blurgh," he groaned. He rolled over, revealing a green grass stain on his shirt. He groaned again.

"Pretty impressive," Jessica teased as she grabbed her water bottle and plopped down next to him. "That was fun," she said gamely.

"Fun," he repeated, still on his back. "You're pure, ponytailed evil, Tuttle."

"All the better to make varsity," she replied with satisfaction. "You're an excellent loser. And an even better skinny-dipper, one hopes." She looked across the yard, wondering how to bring up Liam.

"Why'd you leave the bonfire so early?" Connor asked suddenly, sitting up.

"Um, Lara wanted to go." *Because your brother was maybe hitting on my cousin*, she silently added. "I had fun. What about you?"

He shrugged. "It was all right. Some wasted summer kids tried picking a fight, but they ended up passing out. Did you see it?"

"No, missed that, unfortunately." Jessica leaned back on her elbows, the sun beating down on her dirt-streaked legs. This was the perfect opening. "What's Liam up to today?"

"Working on his Mustang."

"Oh." Strike one. Jessica was clueless about cars. "You guys play lacrosse together?" she asked ultracasually.

"Nah." Strike two. "He kind of sucks at it, and he gets pissy when he loses. He'd rather stay in and fix junk."

Well, so much for having sports in common. But surely there was something else they shared, Jessica just had to find it. She stared up at the blue sky, where puffy white clouds were slowing making their way out to sea.

"We're going to have a few friends over sometime soon, nothing big," Conner said after a silent moment. He pulled a few strands of grass from the ground and threw them at her head. "Would you want to come?"

"Watch it!" Jessica shook the pieces of grass off. "Just for that, I'm going to insist on special treatment — *if* I show up," she teased. But she felt a bolt of excitement at getting to see Liam at a party again.

"Cool." Connor got up and brushed himself off. "Good practice," he told her, tossing some more grass her way. "You'll definitely make varsity by the end of this summer. Maybe even the guys' team."

She brushed the grass off her shirt and smiled a big *you-can't-bother-me* smile. "Thanks for coming over. Let me know when you're ready to put on your little show. I'll bring my camcorder."

Connor took off at a jog down the driveway, but she noticed his lacrosse stick propped up against a tree. "You forgot your stick!"

"Same time tomorrow," he shouted, jogging backward. He nearly tripped over a branch, but caught himself and raised his hands in victory.

Jessica laughed and waved. She hugged herself as she watched him disappear behind the trees, then headed in for a shower. A couple more training/recon sessions with Connor, and she'd be more than ready for her second shot with Liam. Jessica Tuttle was a lot of things — little sister, star athlete, girl with a crush — but she definitely was not a quitter.

"Excuse me, there's a hair in my risotto."

Lara leaned over to see where the customer pointed, and took the plate off the lacquered table. "I'm so sorry, I'll have the kitchen make you another." She took the offending risotto into the kitchen and dumped it in a plastic bin.

"I need a rush seafood risotto, and this time, hold the hair!" she shouted to the cooks. One nodded and banged a pot onto the stove. Another slammed a bunch of full plates onto the counter that separated them and pointed at her.

Lara swept out of the kitchen backward, holding two plates and balancing a third on her forearm. She set them down in front of the waiting couple and their cute little boy. "Will there be anything el —"

A glob of hot macaroni and cheese smacked her dead in the forehead and began to slowly slide down her cheek. The toddler clapped his hands and shrieked with laughter, evidently proud of his aim. The father shook his head and turned back to his crab cakes as the mother murmured a loving rebuke at her little angel, hurrying to pluck a wet wipe from her bag to clean his cheesy, chubby hands.

Lara stifled a groan and caught Drew's sympathetic eye from a few tables down. She smiled weakly and darted to the bathroom, but not before being asked to take a picture of the group at another table. Lara looked in the slightly foggy mirror as she cleaned the food off her face. Pieces of her short black hair were stuck to her forehead with sweat, and her blue eyes looked sleepy. *I need a vacation from my summer vacation.* Taking a deep breath, she opened the bathroom door and grimly headed back into the fray.

Four hours later, Lara closed her last check and sighed with relief. The Saturday dinner rush was ten times harder than she'd expected, and there were moments she was convinced it would never end.

"Rough day?" Zoe gently moved Lara away from the computer so she could print out the check for her remaining table.

Lara began wiping down the waiters' station. "I can't believe it got so busy. And man, people can be *mean*."

Zoe clucked sympathetically. "You'll get used to it," she said, checking the total. "It's only been a few days. The summer people can be a little obnoxious sometimes."

"I take offense to that," Drew declared, popping his head over the partition between the station and the next booth.

"You're right," Lara agreed sweetly. "You're obnoxious *all* the time."

Zoe offered her a high five, and the girls slapped hands, giggling.

"I'll be in the corner licking my wounds," Drew said with a sniffle.

"Beach tonight?" Zoe asked them.

"Magic words." Lara nodded, leaning against the back of a booth.

"I can't say no to an evening with two lovely ladies," Drew said, slinging an arm around each of them. Lara rolled her eyes at Zoe, hoping her nonchalance was convincing. No matter how hard she'd tried, she couldn't push her feelings for Drew in the *friend* direction.

"Actually, it'll be *three* lovely ladies. Kate's coming," Zoe continued. "But you'll have some competition, Drew — I invited my friend James."

"Okay," Lara said, and Drew shrugged. Kate, the red-headed hostess, had immediately warmed up to Lara when she discovered that Drew was her cousin. It turned out she was actually pretty nice, as long as you weren't in competition.

After finishing their cleanup, the four of them started for the beach. It was a calm, clear night, and Lara was fascinated by the number of stars in the black Maine sky.

"It reminds me of when I was little and I spilled glitter on the rug," Lara observed to Drew, who had paused next to her. She barely came up to his shoulders. "My mom was so pissed. It took months to vacuum all of it up, and you can still see some twinkles once in a while."

"A twinkly floor actually sounds kind of cool," Drew remarked as they followed behind Zoe and Kate. He was wearing worn cords and had shoved his hands into the pockets of his dark hoodie. Despite his otherwise careless style, his red-and-black sneakers were pristine, and Lara had even surreptitiously watched him wipe them down with a dishcloth today.

She pointed at them. "What's with those?"

He looked down. "Huh?"

"Your sneakers. They're just *begging* for me to step on them."

He sprang away from her in alarm. "These are original, mint-condition Jordans! The very first Air Jordans ever produced. You're practically desecrating them just by looking at them."

"If they're so precious, why are you wearing them to work?" Lara scoffed.

Drew's expression shifted from outraged to sheepish. "My feet were killing me after that first day," he confessed. "These were the only sneakers I brought. It hurt me deeply to take them out of the box."

"I never knew you were such a fashionista," Lara said airily. "Next time I have sartorial trouble, I'll remember to consult you."

Drew laughed and shook his head. "You're so dead." He came after her, and Lara tried to dodge him, but her long peasant skirt slowed her down. He caught her by the waist and attempted to tickle her, but Lara remained stoic.

"Sorry, you're wasting your time," she told him. "I'm immune."

He lifted his head, perplexed. "What are you, some kind of freak?"

She raised an eyebrow. "I think we both know the answer to that."

As always, the air between them crackled with energy.

"Hello? Don't make me come back there," Zoe warned. She and Kate had stopped and were watching them curiously.

Red-faced, Drew and Lara quickly stepped apart and joined them. Zoe led them to a spot far from the pier and the crowds. A guy with brown hair and soft brown eyes was waiting by a small fire. When he stood up, Lara noticed that he was actually pretty cute. She was grateful to find her cute guydar was back to normal after its recent malfunction.

"Everyone, James. James, everyone." Zoe gestured in James's direction and sat down by the fire. Lara plopped down between James and Zoe, leaving Drew between Kate and Zoe. "James is a lifeguard up at the club," Zoe added.

"You probably have your fair share of monsters there, too," Lara offered.

He laughed while she related the mac-and-cheese episode from that afternoon. James was funny and easy to talk to, but Lara kept glancing over at Drew, who seemed to enjoy being sandwiched by two pretty girls. Kate's giggling grated on Lara's nerves. When she couldn't stand it any longer, she excused herself to gather wood for the fire.

"I'll go with you." Zoe followed Lara to the woods at the edge of the beach. "I think James is into you," she said when they were out of earshot of the group.

"Um," Lara busied herself gathering a few twigs.

Zoe pressed her case. "He's been talking to you all night. Are you getting a vibe?"

"I dunno." She wondered what was going on at the fire, whether Kate was resting her hand on Drew's knee or making that annoying faux-coy face.

"Well, think about it," Zoe said with a touch of

impatience. "He's cute and he's really sweet. And a good friend of mine, so I can totally vouch for him. He really deserves someone as cool as you," she added.

"He's great," Lara agreed, trying to muster up enthusiasm she didn't have. "But I don't really know him."

Zoe flashed her a sly smile. "Leave that to me."

"Thanks," Lara said weakly, even though the idea made her nervous. She gathered some sticks and returned to the fire with Zoe. The other three hadn't budged from their original positions, and there were only a couple of beers left. Lara was about to sit down again, but Drew stood up and yawned, stretching his arms high above his head.

"I'm beat," he announced. "Thanks for the beers, James."

Zoe and Kate protested, but he shook his head. "Coming, Lara?"

"Sure." She hugged Zoe and Kate, and smiled at James. "Nice meeting you."

James immediately jumped up from the sand and kissed her cheek. "I'll see you around?"

"Sure. Later, everyone." Lara waved. Drew finished his good-byes and got in step beside her.

Lara and Drew shuffled down East Shore Road, silent except for the sound of their sneakers against the sandy street.

"What's wrong?" he asked, cutting into the quiet.

Lara inhaled deeply, hoping the clean air would clear her head. The gentle melody of crickets did nothing to relax her.

"Nothing," she lied.

"Well, something's wrong. . . ." He kicked at some pebbles, which went skittering into a pile of sand.

"I don't know. It was a little weird seeing you with Kate," she finally admitted. "I'm not really sure what to feel."

"I know what James wants you to feel," Drew said, laughing a little. He glanced up at the night sky and the light of the moon reflected on his face. "He was practically drooling."

She gave him a little shove and he nearly lost his footing. "I'm serious," he said, looking at her.

"So am I." She stopped in the middle of the road. She wasn't sure why.

He stopped, too, and looked at her seriously. They had passed the pier, and Lara could see the deck lights of their houses in the distance. Her heart began to pound. Drew held out his hand, and because she didn't know what else to do, she took it.

"I want to show you something," he told her, leading her to an outcropping of boulders.

The moon's reflection glittered on the water's surface, and waves lapped quietly at the shore. It was beautiful.

"So what happened to forgetting it ever happened?" Drew leaned back against the rock face. She stared straight ahead at the water, but she could sense him looking at her.

Lara smiled to herself. "I forgot to forget."

"Me, too," he said quietly.

That's when Lara knew. She was falling for him. Like seriously, truly falling for him. She'd *been* falling ever since that first day, before they knew they were cousins. *Step*cousins. If that even counted.

She looked up at his face, wondering if she could tell him how she really felt. Hoping he felt the same way.

Without breaking eye contact, Drew put his hand on the small of her back. He drew her forward slowly, giving her every chance to pull away. But she didn't. They kissed, their lips and tongues moving in perfect rhythm. Lara wrapped her arms around Drew's neck as he deepened the kiss. And then she knew: He was falling for her, too.

12

The amusement park was packed with Saturday night revelers. Tinny pop songs blasted from each ride's speaker system, and the gaudy neon lights made it hard to think. Greer loved it. Compared to sleepy Pebble Beach, Funville USA actually lived up to its name.

"So is this field trip a reward for knowing my knots?" Greer asked Brady as they walked.

"You did pretty well today," Brady acknowledged. "But who's to say this is a reward? Maybe I'm going to strand you on the Pirate Ship."

She scrutinized his face. "You don't seem like a Pirate Ship kind of guy. Maybe — Ferris wheel?"

"You got me. The Pirate Ship makes me want to hurl,"

Brady confessed. "Plus, you can see the ocean from the top of the Ferris wheel."

"As if you don't see it every single day," Greer pointed out. But it sounded nice. And, more important, romantic. "Ferris wheel it is. But first, the games. Then funnel cakes. And we have to do the haunted house."

Brady laughed. "Whoa there. Is this your first amusement park?"

"We're sort of deprived of Ferris wheels in Manhattan," she explained.

"Then we'll go twice," Brady declared gallantly.

Greer grabbed his hand and eagerly pulled him toward the games. When she'd suggested an outing after their lesson, Brady had hesitated. He'd awkwardly explained that he wasn't looking to date anyone, and she reassured him she just wanted to do something fun. That part was true. She just happened to think it would be fun to snag Brady, whether or not he was looking to get involved.

Greer paid for her own games to prove they were just there as friends, but allowed Brady to buy a funnel cake. She was predictably horrible at shooting basketballs, but Brady won the ringtoss and gave her his large, stuffed lobster as consolation.

"You know they make those hoops supersmall so the ball can't possibly go in," she complained, taking a bite of her funnel cake. They were walking toward the Ferris wheel, the last thing on their Funville to-do list.

Brady snickered.

"What?" she demanded. "It's true!"

"It's not that. You, uh, have some powdered sugar on your nose," he told her.

She grabbed the claw of the stuffed lobster and wiped it off. Brady looked pained. "That lobster was really hard to win, you know."

Greer smiled apologetically. "Just breaking him in."

After waiting in a short line, the Ferris wheel attendant turned out to be a kid from Brady's class, so they got on for free. Settling into the two-person seat, Greer was sorry that this was their last stop for the evening. Brady was turning out to be an extra-cute, extra-sweet challenge.

"So, it wasn't so terrible hanging out with me, was it?" she asked him teasingly as their car began to rise.

"It was all right." He shrugged noncommittally and then smiled. "I still have your fingernail marks on my arm from that haunted house ride, though."

Greer laughed. "That *Exorcist* girl was freaky, admit it. And aren't you supposed to be kind to me, on account of being my teacher and all?" She swatted him with the lobster.

"You're right. I'm supposed to be positive with my students." He paused, and Greer sat back, pretending to pout.

"I mean it. You were very cute," Brady said, turning toward her.

She met his gaze then, the dark ocean glistening behind them on the horizon. The distant screams of kids on the Pirate Ship mixed with the music from the carousel. Brady leaned toward her, and their lips finally met, softly at first. The kiss intensified, and it was only when their car descended to ground level that they finally broke apart, each breathing a little heavily. They smiled at each other.

"That was an awesome view," she said after a moment.

Brady just smiled and kissed her again.

When Greer got home, she was still giddy with the unexpected success of her day. Sure, she'd set out to win Brady over — he was the ultimate challenge, after all — but all it had taken was one "Oh, I'm not looking for a boyfriend," a few smiles, and a Ferris wheel ride and he was putty in her hands.

Practically floating up the stairs to her bedroom, she glimpsed the light coming from under Jessica and Lara's door.

"You guys up?" she asked, opening the door. She glanced inside and found Jessica on her bed, poring over an *Allure*. She was swinging her feet back and forth slowly.

"Where's Lara?" Greer asked, sitting on Lara's bed, which was the bottom bunk. She looked around. Jessica's sports equipment was scattered around, along with Lara's books and CDs.

"She was working tonight — not back yet," Jessica said in a clipped tone. She eyed Greer suspiciously. "What's up with *you*?"

"Nothing, why?"

"You just look kind of . . . happy," Jessica observed.

Greer shrugged. "Is that so weird?"

"Well, it's not your usual —" she stopped. "Anyway, what's up?"

"I went to Funville with Brady, my sailing instructor," Greer told her cousin, trying to keep the excitement out of her voice. "He was supposed to be my summer project — a challenge — but I guess he couldn't help himself. . . ." She sighed.

"Well, look at you." Jessica gestured toward Greer's supershort red Proenza Schouler romper, cinched tight with a wide brown belt and sky-high platforms. "I mean, no offense . . ."

Greer frowned. So what if she was wearing something a little revealing? She picked up a rubber lacrosse ball from the floor and chucked it at her cousin's bed. "We hung out all night before he kissed me," she said a little defensively. "And we just kissed. Nothing more."

"Do you think he likes you?"

"I don't know," Greer said honestly. She thought so,

but she couldn't help wondering if it had been a one-time make-out session. "He asked me to a party next week, so I guess we'll see then." Greer got up. This conversation was killing her high.

Jessica looked up at her with wide eyes. "I think you like him more than you're saying." She shrugged.

It was a simple statement, but it took Greer by surprise. "Whatever," was all she could think to say in response.

Greer knitted her brow as she walked to her own room and changed into her nightie. Jessica might be naive and inexperienced, but she wasn't dumb. The last time Greer really liked someone, it didn't exactly end well. She'd found out her boyfriend was cheating on her with a *freshman*. After that humiliation, she had refused to let herself fall for anyone. It had been a system that served her well.

Wrapped in her expensive sheets, she stared at the ceiling, willing Brady to call or even text good night. The minutes ticked by, and a strange feeling settled over her. She couldn't remember the last time she'd actually waited for a guy to call — she'd already won her challenge, so what did she care if Brady got in touch?

The trouble was, she did.

13

Squinting into the sun, Jessica could see Connor trotting up the beach in his usual uniform of cargo shorts with a T-shirt. She noticed that she wasn't the only one watching him — nearly every girl turned her head as he passed by. Connor was definitely cute, but in a little-brother, big-eyed sort of way. Not Jessica's type.

They'd moved their practices to the late afternoon because of the heat, but that wasn't going to help much today. She left the burning deck to hunt down some cold drinks. Their drills had been getting even more intense lately, and she needed to fuel up in advance. Just as she extracted two bottles of Gatorade from the fridge, she heard Connor reach the deck.

"You're a lifesaver," he groaned as she tossed him one

of the bottles. She joined him at an umbrella table. "You still up for coming over tonight?"

"Yeah, but Greer and Lara can't make it." She feigned a careless tone. "Is Liam going to be there?" She'd been quizzing Connor about Liam regularly, but hadn't really found out anything useful. It was getting harder to think of questions that were basic enough to pass as bored curiosity, and they never led to the long, revealing conversations she was hoping for.

"Yeah, he's getting the beer," Connor answered shortly. He got up, grabbing his Gatorade. "Let's go."

Jessica led the way through the house and into the front yard, wondering if something was bugging him today. He usually kidded around until she suggested they start. She retrieved their sticks and balls from the garage, and they practiced scooping up ground balls. When they moved on to checking drills, Jessica grew increasingly frustrated with Connor's halfhearted efforts to steal the ball.

"You don't have to baby me," she finally told him. "And I'm not going to get better if you won't try."

Connor looked uncomfortable. "It's not like you can really check in girls' lacrosse, anyway," he retorted coolly.

"I'm not asking you to tackle me, but my stick doesn't have feelings."

He exhaled loudly. "Fine."

In the next play, he lunged to knock the ball out of her

pocket with his lacrosse stick, accidentally elbowing her solidly in the chest. She fell onto her butt, her hip slamming into the hard grass.

"God, I'm so sorry. Are you okay? I'm sorry —" Connor knelt down next to her, concern darkening his steel-gray eyes.

"I'm fine. Really." Jessica smiled to show him she was okay. She was relieved that they weren't snarking at each other anymore — she hated fighting with her friends. He helped her up and looked contrite as she dusted herself off. "That was really good. I'll have to remember that one for my first game."

A reluctant smile emerged on his face. "Let's quit for the day. People should be heading over soon, anyway."

And I'll be seeing Liam soon.

Leaving Connor on the deck with another Gatorade, Jessica darted upstairs with her heart racing. She took a quick shower and put on a flippy skirt and a tank top, the best she could do in such oppressive heat. When she slid back the glass door and stepped out onto the deck, Connor looked a little shocked.

"You look so . . ." He trailed off.

"What?" she asked, wondering if she'd put something on backward, or her tank was see-through or something.

"Just nice, is all," he told her, and then glanced down at the deck.

She was pleased, and her damp blonde hair felt cool against her neck. "Thanks. I'm sure you'll look pretty good, too, once you take a shower."

He laughed and they started for his house, which was just a few minutes' walk down Peachtree Road. Connor brought her downstairs to the basement, where a few tanned people were lounging on a blue-and-white-striped sofa and chairs.

"I'll be back in a minute, Jessica," Connor said. "Hey, Sandy, come meet my lax buddy," he called to a petite blonde across the room before heading back upstairs.

"I'm Sandy," she introduced herself, walking closer. She had friendly green eyes. "Are you Connor's girlfriend?"

Jessica smiled and the two girls sat down on an empty love seat. "Just friends," she replied, wondering when Liam would appear.

Sandy sighed. "He's cute though, isn't he?"

Before she could answer, Liam thundered down the stairs, grinning.

"What are you two whispering about over here?" Liam asked, coming over to the love seat and squeezing in beside Jessica. She felt her pulse spike. "Girl secrets?"

Sandy giggled. "We're just wondering why your brother's still single," she told him.

"Oh, that dude is beyond help," Liam moaned. "I tried hooking him up a few times, but he's a lost cause."

"Unlike you!" Sandy laughed. Jessica smiled stiffly. *What did that mean?*

"Hey, be nice. I'm not a bad guy." Liam put his arm around Jessica affectionately. "You're going to give Jess here the wrong idea." *Wrong idea?* He squeezed her shoulder. "How've you been, anyway?"

His hazel eyes scanned her face. At this close distance, she could see tiny flecks of green and gold. He was so handsome it almost hurt to look away.

"Connor said you got the Jet Ski running," she mentioned with extreme casualness, studying her flip-flops. "I think you owe me a lesson."

Liam nodded. "Sure. When I get back after July Fourth?"

"Great," she replied as he stood up and grabbed two Wii remotes from the table.

"Listen up, people," he said to the group, and someone turned the music down. "Loser drinks after each point."

Sandy protested. "I suck at this game!"

Liam grinned. "Exactly." Sandy sat back, laughing, and Jessica shot her a look. Was there something going on between her and Liam? She wished Connor would come back so she could try to furtively ask him. "Okay, loser drinks after losing," Liam went on. "We'll do it tournament style, like the pros. First up?"

Jessica sank back into the couch with a beer, laughing halfheartedly while two guys energetically duked it out with their little plastic controllers. She was already on her second beer when Connor came down, his hair wet, and sat next to her.

"Hey," he said, stealing her beer and taking a sip. He smelled like plain soap.

In front of them, the winner took a bow while the loser tossed the remote to Connor. He caught it and won the match easily, which made it Jessica's turn. She took her position next to him.

"Wait, wait. She doesn't have a Mii yet," Liam called from the couch. "Let me see that remote."

She waited nervously as he scrolled through possible hairstyles and colors, wondering what he'd make her look like. Would her Mii be more Anna Kournikova or vintage Martina Navritalova? He finally settled on a blonde ponytail and a cute little all-white outfit. Jessica tried not to smile too broadly or blush.

"Okay," he said, returning the remote with a wink. "Now you can play."

Butterflies zoomed around her stomach. She turned back to the TV and growled to Connor, "You're going down, buddy."

He smirked. As with lacrosse, they were evenly matched, with the point going first to Connor, then Jessica like clockwork. Soon, the room was split between their supporters. At match point, she slammed the ball over the net, too far for Connor to return. There was a collective holding of breath as it landed dangerously close to being out-of-bounds. Jessica bowed in triumph as the room erupted in cheers, and she felt Liam's eyes on her.

After that, Jessica easily defeated Sandy, who laughed off her loss. This was Jessica's kind of party — nothing like a little friendly competition to make her feel comfortable. Liam stepped up next, and as they waited for the game to load, he smiled that amazing smile.

"Be gentle with me," he joked.

Suddenly, she remembered what Connor had said about Liam being a sore loser. She bit her lip, thinking hard.

When the game started, it was her turn to serve. Instead of the fast ace she'd been killing everyone else with, she hit a long stroke in Liam's direction. He returned it easily and they volleyed until she hit the ball into the net. The room groaned.

The rest of the match didn't take long. Jessica won a game, then lost the next, and the next after that. It was all very intentional, of course, and she caught a quizzical look on Connor's face more than once. Finally, in the fourth set, Jessica missed a volley on match point. Liam flashed the victory sign high above his head, the Wiimote dangling from his wrist. "I'm number one!" he shouted. Jessica tried her best to look like a shamefaced loser, and sat down next to Sandy.

"Oh, no, you don't," Liam swooped down on her. "You lost, baby. Take your medicine."

She accepted the beer from him and drank it in three huge gulps. Then she wiped her cherry ChapSticked lips with the back of her hand.

"Yes!" he exclaimed, kissing her loudly on the cheek. He turned to one of his friends. "I love this girl!"

Okay, so she'd lost something on purpose — something she never did — but she'd just won a kiss from the cutest guy she'd ever met. Jessica felt happiness wash over her like warm sunshine. Her Liam plan was working.

14

"Good God, how much underwear does one person need?" Lara grumbled. She was trying vainly to close a shallow drawer that was overstuffed with Greer's lingerie.

"Hopefully enough that I won't have to do laundry," Greer said testily.

"The three of us are going to have so much fun!" Jessica cried enthusiastically from the depths of the closet. "Like a slumber party every night."

Greer groaned — this was a nightmare. After Jessi's dad's college roommate decided to join them for a few weeks, she'd been forced out of her private room and into this hellhole. But apart from taking a room at the Pebble Beach Inn for the rest of the summer, she didn't really have a choice.

She sat down on the only chair. With the beds taking up most of the room, the other furniture was a dresser and a tiny desk. It was like a very new, shiny, white prison cell, except she was pretty sure that even convicts got their own toilets. She eyed the top bunk resentfully. "How do I even get up there?"

"There's a ladder on the side," Lara pointed. "It's the penthouse, so you'll feel right at home."

Greer shot her a look.

"Let's go into town tonight," Jessica coaxed, trying on a pair of Greer's peep-toe wedges. "Just us. We need to celebrate Greer moving in."

"I'm in," Greer sighed. She didn't need to be persuaded to get out of this cell. "Let's hit the clubs. Wait, does Pebble Beach even *have* a club?"

"Yeah, there's Cove down by the surf shop," Lara offered. "Zoe said it was decent."

Greer closed her eyes, mentally planning her outfit.

"Any news on Brady?" Jessica asked.

She snapped her eyes open. "No, my next lesson's tomorrow."

Jessica giddily filled Lara in on the details of Greer's night on the pier, and then finished with five little words: "I think she likes him."

Greer rolled her eyes. Okay, so maybe. She hadn't been able to stop thinking about Brady since their kiss. He had to cancel their last lesson because his sister had a youth regatta she was sailing in, and he needed to cheer her on. It was all so nauseatingly sweet she could vomit.

"Whatever," Greer said dismissively. "I'm not looking for anything serious — if he can't help but fall all over himself to get me, who am I to judge?"

Lara scoffed. "I'm sure it also helps that you look like . . ."

"What?" Greer demanded, pulling her long dark hair into a messy ponytail. She blinked her heavily lashed eyes innocently.

"You!" both girls said in unison.

"Oh, please," she said, waving a hand around. She was used to people talking about how pretty she was, but she liked to think that maybe Brady actually saw something in her besides her long legs and perfect complexion. "What's going on with *you*, anyway?" Greer nodded at Lara. "You never talk about guys." She paused. "Or girls," she added, just to be open-minded. Lara *did* have that short little pixie do.

Lara chuckled, though her face did seem a little pink. "There just isn't much to tell. I'm working all the time."

"There's always *somebody* worth talking about," Greer maintained. The only person that Lara ever seemed to talk about was her coworker Zoe. . . . "Maybe someone at Ahoy?" she asked leadingly.

Lara looked away and rearranged the pillows on her bed. "Um, I met this guy James the other night," she said after a moment. "He was really cute."

"Oh?" Well, so much for that theory. Greer shuffled over to her overstuffed underwear drawer and pulled it open.

"Yeah, why didn't you mention him before?" Jessica challenged.

"It's nothing. We just met. He's a friend of Zoe's." Lara babbled quickly. She smoothed down her duvet in quick strokes. "Who knows if I'll ever see him again."

"Hmmm." Greer pulled out her underthings and set to folding them. She glanced over at Lara, squinting. The poor girl was practically sweating, and Greer was beginning to have a theory as to why. She stood up and adjusted her tank top.

"Anyway," Lara said loudly. "Let's talk about important stuff. Like if Greer snores or not. Because I can't sleep under those circumstances."

Greer flung a pair of zebra-striped boy shorts at Lara. "I've never had any complaints before!"

Jessica laughed, grabbing one of Greer's nighties from the pile on the floor. "Have you seen her pj's? They're totally X-rated."

"No wonder she never gets complaints," Lara sputtered.

Greer smirked. And as Lara and Jessica began counting off the number of times they'd witnessed Greer giving the bitchface to some poor smitten boy, she had to admit that hanging out with her cousins wasn't completely boring. Neither were the sailing lessons. Or any minute spent with Brady.

Maybe this summer wasn't such a disaster after all.

15

Lara's head split open and her brains fell onto her pink flowered sheets. At least, that's what it felt like as she failed in her attempt to roll over. What had happened to her? *Oh, yeah. Screwdrivers happened.*

As soon as the girls had arrived at Cove, Greer had gotten to work flirting with the extremely cute bartender. Consequently, he'd poured them free drinks all night. Lara opened a heavy eyelid and saw a Jessica-like shape across the room, sprawled half-in and half-out of her bed. Greer must have been in the top bunk, but Lara couldn't imagine moving enough to look for her. Her eye closed again.

Why had she woken up? There was a reason nagging at the back of her mind. *Right. Work.* She tried to go back to sleep but the knowledge wouldn't go away. She staggered out of bed and into the shower, hoping the hot water would chase away the pain.

Her cousins were still asleep when she came out of the bathroom, and Lara tried her best not to make noise, despite her reduced mental and physical faculties. She crawled around in her towel, trying to identify any of her own clothes, but it was impossible to tell in the dim light. They'd gotten dressed for the club a little too enthusiastically, and now most of her stuff was on the floor. Finally, she picked up two dark garments that had a very good chance of being a top and a bottom. Grabbing her bag and her shoes, she stumbled out the door. When she saw the clothes she'd grabbed, her headache intensified. Greer's skimpy black tank top had SPOIL ME written on the front in swirly pink glitter. The denim miniskirt wasn't nearly as offensive, except that Lara had never worn a miniskirt in her life. *Whatever*. She was late. She pulled the clothes on and ran out the door.

By the time she reached Ahoy, Lara wasn't sure if she was going to make it through the day. She had a few minutes before her shift started, so she sat in a booth with a huge glass of water and put her head on the weathered table. It was the only way to reduce the throbbing.

"Rough night?" Drew's voice sounded far away, and she was vaguely aware of him sliding in the booth across from her. She'd managed to avoid being alone with him since their midnight makeout on the beach last week, even though it was never far from her mind. Even through her misery, her heart beat faster at the sound of his voice.

"You could say that." She couldn't pick her head up.

"I hope you're not being a bad influence on my little sister."

Lara snorted, which made her grimace in pain. "She's partly to blame for my condition, so no."

"Be right back."

Lara didn't respond. After what seemed like mere seconds, he returned and she heard the thud of a plate being placed on the table next to her head. She sat up and looked. In front of her was a steaming-hot breakfast burrito, stuffed with egg, cheese, and sausage. Along with two Advils.

"My miracle cure," Drew assured her. "Trust me."

As much as she didn't want to eat, Lara felt a sudden gnawing in her stomach. She threw the Advils into her mouth and washed them down with a big gulp of water. She picked up the burrito and bit into it, instantly grateful for the hot, greasy goodness. She shot Drew a thankful look. "How'd you score this?"

Drew shrugged. "The cooks owed me one. I hope you're worth it."

She pointed at her tank top. "This says it all." She saw the look on his face change, and suddenly felt awkward. She hunched over her burrito. "Thanks, by the way."

"We shouldn't be too busy. I'll handle most of the tables if you want to chill."

Lara was touched by his concern. "I'll be fine after this," she said, indicating the magic burrito. "Thanks."

Richard came out and walked over. "Morning, mates. It'll be slow today — the brief calm before the July Fourth frenzy — so we'll be closing early to do inventory. I'll need you both to handle the pantry. The cooks will do the fridges and freezer tomorrow when the deliveries come in."

Lara nodded. The news couldn't have come on a better day. She hadn't been looking forward to the prospect of waiting on loud people.

"Cheers. I'll be out the rest of the day, but call my mobile if the place burns down. Zoe's not in today, so, Lara, you lock up." With a sunny smile, he left.

After clocking in, the day went by quickly, which Lara was grateful for. Drew took the majority of tables while Lara did all the side work, and he split the tips with her at the end. When the last cook had gone, Lara locked the door and took out the inventory list that Richard had left.

"Kidney beans." Drew was sitting on a step stool and calling off items, while Lara checked the racks and answered with the number of cans. "Feeling better?"

Lara found the beans and counted. "Four. Yeah, I'm feeling vaguely human again."

He made a mark on the list. "Chopped tomatoes. You're a champ for coming in at all."

"Yeah, well, today's check might mean the difference between AC or no AC in my car. Three big ones."

Drew frowned. "There should be five."

She crouched down and peered around the low shelf. "Nope. Three."

"All right. Mayo."

Lara hunted around and finally spotted the enormous white jars on the top shelf. She stood on her tiptoes but couldn't see if any were hiding in the back. She commandeered Drew's stool and stood on it, counting. She looked back at him. "There's sev — hey!"

He was blatantly staring at the ridiculously short hem of her skirt. And with her up on the stool, he was getting an eyeful. She grabbed a small plastic jar of horseradish and threw it at him. He caught it easily but didn't even have the decency to look ashamed. He grinned, forcing her to look for the next smallest object she could hurl at him. She strained to reach a can of cranberry sauce, when she suddenly felt a dangerous wobble.

Oh, no.

The step stool tipped over in slow motion. Lara frantically grabbed at a shelf to keep from falling. But instead of steadying her, the shelf came off the wall with a jerk. She yelped in fear as she fell, then felt strong arms gripping her as Drew caught her. Her forward momentum brought both of them crashing to the floor, with large jars of mayonnaise thudding heavily around them.

Ow. She'd banged her elbow hard on the tile floor, but at least it wasn't her head. She started laughing, partly out of fear and partly out of relief. She peered at Drew, who was lying underneath her, shaking his head. His arms were still around her.

She stopped laughing. "Are you okay?"

He looked at her. "I'll live. You?"

"Yeah, thanks. You're my hero today." Neither of them made any effort to get up.

"It was the least I could do. I was the one looking up your skirt, after all."

She nodded, her chin rubbing against his chest. "True. When did you become such a perv?"

"When did you start dressing like jailbait?" he countered.

"Touché." And then she kissed him. She couldn't help it.

He kissed her back, deeply enough to send electricity to her fingertips. Then, as she pulled back, she caught a sudden movement from the corner of her eye and turned her head to see Zoe's shocked face in the open doorway. Lara couldn't move as Zoe's eyes involuntarily took in Drew lying underneath her, then glanced back at Lara.

We're cousins, Lara had told her.

"I — I'm sorry," Zoe stammered as she vanished from the doorway. Lara quickly jumped up and followed after, catching her friend just as she was about to leave the restaurant.

Zoe spun around and held up her hands, palms out. "Look, what you do is your own business. I don't want to know!"

"No, you have the wrong idea," Lara said forcefully. "It wasn't —"

"Whatever. I just needed my paycheck and now I'm out." Zoe swung open the door and was gone.

Lara stared after her, processing the utter revulsion on Zoe's face. She'd never felt so repulsive. It was all too easy to see herself through Zoe's disgusted eyes. What *was* she doing? If anyone in their family found out —

Hearing a sound behind her, she spun around and saw Drew standing by the kitchen doors, watching her. He came forward, but she backed away from him.

"Lara, I —"

"No," she hissed, her thoughts tangling in confusion. "Not now." She felt the solidity of the front door against her back and curled her hand around the doorknob.

He tried again. "Let's talk about this. Sit —"

"No!" she shouted. She opened the door and ran into the night, bumping blindly into curious people on the street. She didn't look back to see if Drew was following her. She didn't care.

16

"Just give me a sec."

Jessica watched as Greer smoothed the Kérastase UV defense cream into her shiny brown hair. She never failed to use it after lying out in the sun. In the short time since Greer had moved in, Jessica had become fascinated by her various beauty regimens. Her morning routine took the longest — Jessica counted eighteen separate steps before Greer would even venture downstairs.

Jessica was sitting on her bed, inspecting her tan lines. She'd been trying to even out the farmer's tan she'd gotten after going for a six-mile run in a T-shirt, but her strategic sunblock placement didn't seem to be working. "Do I finally get to meet the dreamy sailing instructor tonight?"

Greer nodded, then went over to her luggage, which

still held most of her clothes. She pulled on a pair of expensive-looking jeans and a black shell with tiny ruffles down the front.

She stepped into flat gold sandals and turned to Jessica. "Ready."

Jessica envied Greer's complete confidence in her style, as well as her bulging suitcases. She looked down at her own outfit — a shrunken tee and skinny jeans that didn't cling to her curves like Greer's. Resigned, she got up and followed her coiffed cousin out to the beach.

Dusk had fallen, and they could see the party about a half mile down the beach, by the pier. Jessica wished Lara was with them, but she'd been MIA lately. Jessica wondered if it had anything to do with that James guy — Lara dismissed the idea whenever it came up, but Jessica was beginning to wonder.

At least Connor would be there — and Liam.

Jessica hadn't seen Liam since her Wii "loss," and she was eager to connect with him tonight.

As they approached the party, Jessica could see at least twenty or thirty kids surrounding the small beach fire. She spotted Sandy and some of the guys from the other afternoon in Liam's basement. Then Connor appeared.

"Hey." He gave them both a crooked smile.

"Hey, yourself," Greer answered affectionately. "How's life?"

"Your cousin's been kicking my ass at lacrosse, but I'm man enough to be okay with it," Connor replied. "She cheats, though."

"Do not!" Jessica knuckle-punched him on the shoulder.

"Foul!" He stepped away from her. "I don't know how you live with this immaturity," he complained to Greer.

"Settle down, kids," Greer said drily. "Or get a room."

Jessica couldn't tell if Connor blushed, or if it was the flickering of the fire. She was about to retort when she saw a tall, clean-cut boy coming toward them. "Red alert," she murmured, looking forward to watching Greer deliver another soul-crushing dismissal.

Greer turned as the boy reached their circle, and Jessica watched an unusual expression come over her cousin's face. She looked *happy*.

"Hey, sailor," he said to Greer. He nodded casually at Connor and turned to Jessica, "I'm Brady."

Brady was Ralph Lauren–model good-looking, and standing next to Greer in the haze of firelight, they looked like they belonged in a magazine ad. "Jessica. I'm Greer's cousin."

"Oh, so this is the Jessi I've been hearing about?" Brady asked teasingly.

Jessica tensed when she heard her little-girl nickname.

"What did she say?" she asked, wondering what snarky remarks Greer might have made about her.

He looked up at the starry sky as if trying to recall. "Just that you were this incredible athlete . . . and something about you being smart and fun. I don't really remember details."

Jessica looked at Greer in surprise, but her cousin only shrugged.

He smiled noncommittally and said to Greer, "Want to look for some firewood?"

Greer fluttered her fingers at Jessica as she and Brady walked off beyond the fire. The night had turned pitch-black against the bright flames, and Jessica felt warmed by both the fire and the thought that Greer had said such nice things about her.

Jessica and Connor sat close to the heat and talked about their workout plan for the week. He was going away for the upcoming Fourth of July with his family, and Jessica's mind went straight to Liam.

"Earth to Jessica." Connor was waving a hand in front of her face.

"Oh, sorry," she apologized. "What did you say?"

"Running tomorrow? You know, putting one foot in front of the other really quickly?"

"Yeah, sounds good." She smiled at him, recalling something. "So when are you going to deliver on that skinny-dipping bet?"

He dropped his head into his hands. "I was hoping you forgot about that," he groaned.

"How could I forget about something so embarrassing?" Jessica mocked. "I'll make you a deal. Do it now, while it's dark, and you're off the hook."

Connor looked at the crowd. "Uh, I don't know. My friends —"

"Won't be able to see you," she finished. "But you have to strip on the beach."

He started shaking his head vehemently. "No way, no *way*."

"Otherwise it's tomorrow at three P.M. With lifeguards, families, pretty much the whole town watching."

"God, you're brutal," he muttered.

He shook his head in resignation and slowly walked down toward the ocean. Smiling, Jessica strolled over to Sandy and whispered in her ear. Sandy spun around and spotted Connor heading toward the water, pulling off his shirt.

"Skinny-dip!" Sandy shouted at the top of her lungs and pointed at the barely visible figure in the darkness. "Connor's skinny-dipping!"

All at once, every head turned toward the ocean. Laughter broke out and people ran closer to get a better look. Connor waited until he was right at the water's edge before quickly snatching off his shorts and boxers and running into the water amidst mass catcalls and whistles. His butt, which was about twenty shades lighter than the rest of his body, disappeared into the dark ocean. Jessica laughed until her eyes watered, then made her way to the front of the crowd to blow Connor a kiss as his head bobbed in the waves. Soon other kids were stripping down and dashing into the water. It looked like so much fun that Jessica contemplated joining them, when a pair of large, warm hands suddenly covered her eyes.

"Guess who?"

She smiled, forgetting about everything else. "My fairy godmother?"

"Close. I won't turn you into a pumpkin, though." Liam let go and stood beside her, looking beyond her at the shouting swimmers. "They're crazy."

He laughed and walked back to the fire, prompting her to follow him. They sat down alone in front of the crackling flames. It suddenly occurred to her that this would be the perfect moment, with the perfect boy, for her perfect first kiss. She drew a deep breath.

"Did I tell you how awesome you were the other day?" Liam asked.

Okay, this wasn't kissing, but she'd take it. "No," she said modestly.

"Connor says you've been kicking his ass in workouts. I didn't know you were such an animal on the field," he went on, punching her lightly on the arm.

Cheesy lines about being like an animal elsewhere filled her head, but she shook them away. "I like to keep up with the boys," she said flirtatiously, instead. Even *that* made her blush, but it was worth it to get Liam to really notice her.

"Word." He nodded. "You're like . . . one of the guys."

Wait. One of the guys?

Jessica felt a rush of embarrassment and a prickling behind her eyes. *One of the guys?* Her shoulders slouched forward, like her chest was trying to protect her heart. Which maybe, a little, it was. People were returning to the fire to warm up, their bodies glistening with water. She kept her eyes on the flames and heard the slap of palms as Liam greeted his friends.

"I'll be right back," he said in her ear, and stood.

A hot tear fell then, streaking her check, and she hastily got up and walked in the opposite direction from Liam. She quickly looked around for Greer, but didn't see her among the faces that were walking up from the water.

"Jessica!" She turned at the sound of the male voice, hopeful.

Connor ran to catch up to her, wearing his clothes with water dripping from his hair.

"Done and *done!*" he gasped cheerfully. "Last time I ever bet against *you.*"

Jessica stared at him.

"Hey, are you okay?" he asked, his smile fading away. "You look upset."

She was overwhelmed with emotions, none of them good: Disappointment that Connor wasn't Liam. Misery because of what Liam said. Shame from her tears. There were no words to explain how she felt. So she just turned and started back to Peachtree Road.

17

Greer couldn't keep the smile off her face as Brady led her to the edge of the beach, where the sand gave way to dense trees. They were almost completely hidden from the party, and Greer knew that collecting firewood was the last thing on his mind.

She was right. Brady pulled her close and gently kissed her, his hands on her waist and his stubble brushing against her chin as their tongues touched. Greer felt pleasure race through her. They stayed in the shadows for a while, oblivious to anything else around them, until the shouts and laughter became loud enough to intrude on their privacy. Pulling away from Greer's eager lips, Brady glanced over at the beach and grinned. "They're skinny-dipping."

Greer turned and watched the idiots dive into the ocean. She giggled as some boys did handstands in the water, showing off way more than just their sense of balance. Brady leaned down to grab a few sticks, then took Greer by the hand and led her back to the party. As they passed near the fire, Brady tossed the sticks onto a big pile.

"Is that your cousin?" Brady asked, looking at the other side of the fire.

Greer peered at a couple of silhouettes sitting in front of the bright flames. She thought one was Jessica, and the other could be Connor. She hoped Jessi had finally come to her senses.

"Yeah, with Connor, I think. At least, I *hope*," she corrected.

He smiled down at her. "Connor's a good kid."

"Yeah, he's a cutie. Perfect for Jessi. It's his brother I'm not too fond of."

"Liam?" Brady's lips curled in distaste. "Yeah. He's been with practically every girl in school."

That confirmed her suspicions. "I hope Jessi doesn't have to learn the hard way. She's so innocent, it'll traumatize her."

Brady chuckled.

Greer looked at him quizzically. "What are you laughing at?"

When he didn't stop, she poked him in the ribs. "What?"

"You." Brady inhaled, trying to catch his breath. "Your concern for people's broken hearts is really touching." He started laughing again.

She narrowed her blue eyes at him. "What are you talking about?"

He finally pulled himself together. "I was just thinking of poor Noah." *Great. That again.* If she'd known that that little dork would've come back to haunt her like this, she never would've talked to him at that stupid holiday party.

"He came back from winter break like he won the lottery or something," Brady went on. "He had this crappy camera phone pic of you that he was always flashing around. It was sad, that's all."

Seriously? We're still talking about this?

"Anyway, it's just funny to hear you so worried when you're a professional heartbreaker."

Did Brady honestly just compare her to Liam? If that was really what he thought of her, what was he doing kissing her on Ferris wheels and at beach bonfires?

"Noah was a little over the top," she told him. "I mean, a camera phone pic?" she asked, even though she remembered when they took it. She'd been sitting on a park bench in Central Park, near the entrance to her apartment.

"He always did get a little too into the girls he liked," Brady admitted. "The one before you, she was like this emo goth chick, and he wrote her this song —"

"No way."

Brady started laughing. "It was so bad. He wore these black clothes and the lyrics were all about death and anarchy. He made me tape it!"

Greer grinned evilly. "You've got to let me see that."

Brady shook his head, smiling. "He'd kill me."

"You could put it up on YouTube and say someone stole the tape."

Brady grabbed her hand and kissed it. "I'm a little afraid of you."

Greer felt her heart soften. For someone who had claimed he didn't want to date, he certainly wasn't acting like it. She rolled the word "boyfriend" around in her head, testing its strangeness. But with Brady, everything felt so comfortable and safe. She was a little shocked at herself — she'd started off thinking that Brady was just going to be a fun project, but now. . . . Greer Hallsey in Maine with a *boyfriend*?

She'd done crazier things before.

"So, this no-dating policy of yours . . . is it written in stone?" she hedged.

Brady ducked his head quickly. When he raised it again, she was relieved to see he was smiling. Still holding her hand, he started walking to the water's edge, tugging her gently with him. "I don't know, are you trying to change my mind?"

If he wanted to play games, he picked the wrong girl. Greer was way ahead of him. "No," she answered sweetly.

He stopped walking. "No?"

"I'm just having a good time right now," she said nonchalantly. She knew that nothing infuriated a guy more than indifference. Boys might have a reputation for not wanting commitment, but *they* wanted to be the ones to slow things down.

"Oh, you are, huh?" He gave her an appraising glance. "Who are you having all this fun with?"

"You know . . . Jessi, Lara, other people." She smiled coyly. A cold wind picked up, whipping her long hair across her face.

"Other people," he repeated. He shook his head and squeezed her hand. "No wonder Noah went nuts."

Greer arched an eyebrow. "You're no Noah."

He laughed. "I hope you remember that." He noticed her shivering in her thin silky top. "Let's go talk about this where it's warmer."

They walked back up to the fire. But when they reached the edge of the pit, Brady abruptly dropped her hand. Greer looked up at him, startled. He was staring across the fire at a pretty girl with curly blonde hair who was deep in conversation.

"Excuse me," he mumbled. Without even looking at Greer, Brady marched around the fire.

Greer watched, disbelieving, as he went up to the girl, who greeted his stony hello with a smile and a tight hug. Was *this* the ex-girlfriend, Kaitlyn? She had an apple-pie American look, complete with freckles along the bridge of her nose, that matched Brady's perfectly. Sure, they'd been together for a long time, but did he really have to walk away so coldly?

After a couple of minutes, Brady and Kaitlyn backed away from the bonfire. She watched him motion down the beach with his head, and without so much as a wave good-bye, they were gone.

Greer wasn't the kind of girl to go running after anyone. But, she also wasn't the sort of girl who felt short, stabbing pains in her chest as she watched a guy walk away from her.

Maybe that was because she had always been the one doing the walking.

18

The three packed Tuttle houses buzzed with Fourth of July activity. Lara took refuge in the cousins' messy bedroom, lazily rereading her well-worn copy of *Through the Looking Glass* with her feet propped up on the wall.

"Time to eat," Greer commanded from the doorway, sounding eerily like the Red Queen. "You must experience this feast for yourself."

Lara put down her book. "Pigging out in honor of our forefathers' struggle for freedom," she observed. "How patriotic."

"It's not about the food," Greer replied, entering and hauling her up by one arm. "The heat must be getting to the adults. They're being so bitchy, it's insane. I think they're arguing about what to do with the houses. There's one camp that apparently doesn't think we should come back next summer. Jessica looks about ready to explode."

Intrigued, Lara followed her to the deck, where Jessica was obediently laying out cups and plates. Clusters of Tuttles had congregated at the small tables brought over from the other houses, and Lara noted with mingled relief and disappointment that Drew was not there — Jessica had mentioned that he was visiting their other brother, Jordan, today. The grill was off, for once. Jessica had mentioned that it was a family tradition to take a break from barbecuing on the Fourth. Instead, six-foot-long subs were set out, along with bowls overflowing with potato salad, coleslaw, pasta salad, and sour pickles. Lara and Greer glanced at the long buffet line and went for drinks instead—Diet Cokes.

Jessica had snagged a table, and the three girls sat and sipped quietly, hoping to witness some adult drunkenness. In all the families Lara had been a part of, holidays were reliable for at least one embarrassing familial incident — too many relatives combined with too many drinks made a potent mix. And some of the aunts and uncles were arguing, though about what wasn't clear.

"You know what . . ." Lara started, thinking back to so many families and so many holiday celebrations with people she never saw again. "Let's get out of here."

*　　*　　*

The Mercedes swerved left and right as Greer twisted down the tortuous Maine roads. Her passengers shrieked with fear and laughter as they were pitched against the sides of the convertible. "These lobster rolls better be good!" Lara yelled.

Unbelievably, they made it to Red's in one piece. Lara stumbled out from the backseat and knelt on the ground, murmuring, "Thank you, thank you."

"Don't be such a drama queen," Greer sniffed. She checked her makeup in the rearview mirror, then got out.

Jessica led the way to the shack's service window. "Beth and Ella used to bring me here. I hope they're still as good."

"Well, let's see if it's worth the hype. Three lobster rolls," Greer told the love-struck boy behind the window. Noting his adoring gaze, she pressed her advantage. "And three beers."

The boy nodded and fetched their order. As he handed Greer the heavy tray, he asked, "What's your —"

"No," she said dismissively, dropping cash on the counter. Lara and Jessica giggled at the poor kid's stricken face. They found a table that overlooked the ocean, and Lara suddenly felt ravenous. She quickly bit into the roll and widened her eyes.

"Oh, my God."

"What?" They looked at her, alarmed.

Savoring the sweet lobster and buttery roll, Lara let herself finish her perfect bite before answering. "This is the closest I've ever come to a religious experience."

Jessica beamed and bit into hers. "It's even better than I remember," she breathed.

Skeptically, Greer picked up her roll and took a dainty nibble. "Wow."

The noise of occasional cars passing by blended with the water crashing below to create a rhythmic background sound track to their meal. For a while, the girls focused on eating, delighting in each bite.

As they chewed, Jessica finally asked, "So, Lara, anything you want to talk about?"

Lara shook her head. "Nah."

"It's that James guy you mentioned, isn't it?" Jessica scooped up a dollop of mayo'd lobster from her roll and ate it. "Can't you ask Zoe to hook you up?"

Lara wanted this conversation to end *now*. She hated lying, almost as much as she hated feeling like a hypocrite. "I'll ask her at work tomorrow."

"Problem solved," Greer said. "Next?"

"Um," Jessica ventured. "Liam?" Greer and Lara groaned, even though Lara was relieved the focus was off her.

"I know, I know," she said. "But just listen." She told them about the bonfire and his painful line about her being one of the guys.

"Ouch," Lara said sympathetically. She took another bite, wondering how Drew saw her.

Greer squinted at Jessica. "It's makeover time," she pronounced.

"Hey!" Jessica objected. "I bought new clothes for the summer."

"You asked for advice," Greer reminded her.

"Fine." Jessica rolled her eyes. "Speaking of the bonfire, what about you? I never saw you again after you left with Brady."

Greer looked stonily at her beer bottle. "We had fun. Until his ex-girlfriend showed up."

"Whoa," the two girls said simultaneously.

"Yup." Greer studied her beer. "And he left with her five minutes later."

Lara smiled. "You really like him." She was surprised Greer had let herself get upset over a *guy*. She had a feeling Greer had surprised herself a bit, too.

Greer leveled a look at Lara. "No." She popped the last of the roll in her mouth. "I have another lesson next week, so we'll see what happens."

Twilight was giving way to darkness. Greer wanted to sober up, so the three girls bought ice-cream cones and gathered on Red's deck to watch the fireworks. Soon, bursts of red were lighting up the sky, with booms following seconds later. The girls watched silently as one explosion followed after another, showering the night with bright ribbons of color.

"Happy Independence Day, bitches!" Greer toasted affectionately, raising her cone up high.

"Happy Independence Day," Lara and Jessica repeated, laughing.

In that moment, standing together with Jessica and Greer, Lara didn't feel like an outsider. Looking at her cousins, she felt like part of a real family.

19

"No, no, no . . . and no." Jessica stood in front of the closet, frustrated. The clothes she'd bought before coming to Pebble Beach last month looked so juvenile now, especially next to Greer's designer wardrobe and Lara's unique thrift-store style.

"What's going on?" Greer sauntered into the room, dropping her car keys and huge Chanel sunglasses on the desk. She nudged the pile of clothes by Jessica's feet with a pedicured toe. "Goodwill?" she asked.

"No, that's my keep pile!" Jessica grabbed the clothes and faced her cousin. "I need help."

Greer looked at her expectantly. "Lobster rolls?"

"Not that kind of help." Jessica thought of Greer's outfit that first night at the bonfire, and Liam's reaction to it. Jessica didn't own anything *remotely* like that. Her shorts were more of the polyester variety with racing stripes and elastic waistbands. "But you *did* mention a makeover."

"I did," acknowledged Greer. "Is today the day?"

Jessica paused. She'd mulled over Greer's offer for the past week and had some reservations. She wanted to look more sophisticated, but like herself. Mature, not slutty. Ready to make out, but not make *it*. "Just — can you make sure I'm still recognizable?"

"Don't worry," Greer assured her gleefully. "You're in excellent hands."

Lara walked in as Greer was digging through her luggage, tossing clothes all over the room. "Ooh, can I help fling your clothes around? I bet I'll be really good at it."

Greer flicked a dark lock of hair out of her eyes as Jessica giggled. "No, but you *can* help me help Jessi."

"Jessica," Jessica corrected automatically. Greer rolled her eyes.

"And how are we helping Jessi-*ca*?" Lara asked.

"A makeover." Greer's eyes sparkled. "She wants to be a hottie."

Lara picked her way over to Jessica and sat down on her bed. "You're hot already," Lara reminded her.

Jessica flopped back on her bed. "I just want to see what it's like. To look like a girly-girl instead of a jock."

"Okay, I'm done. Ready?" Greer had stood up with a pile of clothes in her arms. "We're going to have a fashion show, *Project Runway*–style. Lara, you'll be Michael Kors. I'm Heidi."

Ignoring Lara's dirty look, Greer dropped the pile of clothes on Jessica's bed and picked out a pair of skinny jeans and a shimmery, pale gold top that was formfitting except for its wide, blousy sleeves. "These first."

Once Jessica had squeezed into the jeans, Greer tossed her a pair of four-inch red Jimmy Choo platforms. "We're the same size," Jessica marveled.

"Lucky you," Greer replied drily. She clapped her hands. "Okay, let's see it in action."

Jessica rose from her bed, wobbling dangerously. She lived in sneakers, flip-flops, and the occasional ballet flat — these were like stilts. "It hurts."

"Pain is beauty," Greer agreed pleasantly. Lara snickered.

Feeling slightly foolish, Jessica walked tentatively around the room. She turned to face the judges. "Um, guys?"

Greer had tilted her head and was looking at her critically. "You look amazing," she pronounced.

Lara clapped. "Hot mama!"

Jessica flushed, looking down. Her legs seemed to go on for miles. *So this is how Greer does it — it's all in the shoes.*

The next outfit was a tissue-thin minidress in bright kelly green. The V-neckline plunged well below Jessica's B-cups, and the straps were so delicate that she was afraid they'd snap. She presented herself for judgment.

"B plus," Lara commented.

"A minus," Greer corrected. "But if you're uncomfortable, then it's a definite no."

Jessica felt much more like herself on the third try. She put on cargo shorts and a short-sleeved red jacket with matching Louboutins.

"Hot, hot, hot," Lara declared.

"Totally gorgeous." Greer nodded. "Look at yourself."

Jessica faced the mirror and was speechless when she saw her reflection. She looked like a supermodel. She struck a pose for her cousins, and promptly had a magazine thrown at her.

"Time for hair and makeup." Greer got up and brought the chair over to the mirror for Jessica. She worked quickly, showing Jessica her techniques in the mirror.

"Um, *ow*." Jessica was distracted by a painful tweezer attack on her eyebrows. "Oh, Greer, your dad called while you were out. He told my mom you haven't been calling him back?"

Greer paused while rooting in her black vinyl Prada case. "What else did he say?"

"Um, that's it, I think. Oh, and he wanted to know if

you talked to your mom." Jessica had been sitting in the kitchen during the phone call and noticed her mother kept her side of the conversation unusually short.

Greer lined Jessica's eyes, then sat back, evaluating her work. Fixing her gaze on Jessica's lips, she applied color with a tiny brush. "He's having an affair."

Jessica stared at Greer in shock as Lara looked up from her magazine. "What did you say?" She couldn't have heard her right. Not even Greer could drop something like that with so little emotion.

"My father is having an affair with his twenty-one-year-old intern," Greer repeated with exaggerated clarity, her fingers working swiftly.

"H-how do you know?" Jessica stammered. Greer wouldn't meet her eyes, though their faces were just inches apart. She fiddled with Jessica's hair.

"I saw a text from her in his BlackBerry a few months ago." Greer sat back again, satisfied. "You can look now."

Still reeling, Jessica glanced at the mirror and was taken aback. The makeup itself was barely noticeable, but her moss-green eyes were brighter and her skin seemed to glow. With her hair pulled back simply but flatteringly, she still looked like Jessica, but totally gorgeous.

She turned to thank her cousin, but the words lodged in her throat when she saw a tear running down Greer's face. The idea of Greer crying was so ludicrous that Jessica couldn't do anything but open and close her mouth. She got up and stared meaningfully at Lara, who nodded and plopped into the makeover chair.

"My turn," Lara announced to Greer. "Give me something dramatic."

"Um, just a sec," Greer said, her voice muffled as she pressed a tissue to her face. When she looked up, her warning expression was clear. She combed Lara's hair back and rummaged through a selection of makeup brushes.

"My first stepfather cheated on my mom," Lara mentioned as she stared into the mirror. "I was ten. I remember her crying in her room."

Greer didn't say anything as she applied Lara's foundation with a spongy wedge.

"At first I thought that she was talking about my dad. She kept saying, 'How could he do this to me?' which was what she'd said when my dad died." Lara cleared her throat. "Anyway, they got divorced a year later."

"Were you glad they broke up?" Jessica asked. She couldn't imagine dealing with something like that now, much less when she was ten.

Lara nodded. "They argued all the time. I would play outside until it got dark and my mom had to drag me in."

Greer finally spoke again, quietly. "I don't want them to get divorced."

Jessica didn't know what to say. She envied Greer for a million reasons, but this was bigger than perfect hair or endless money. She felt a surge of affection and sympathy for her usually unflappable cousin. "Come with us to Ithaca," she blurted out impulsively.

Greer whipped her head around. She stared at Jessica for a moment, then cracked up.

Jessica's swelling heart shrunk back down to normal size. "Or not."

"No, no," Greer sputtered. "I don't mean it like that. It's just — could you imagine me in Ithaca?"

"All the cute boys from Cornell are there," Jessica said defensively.

Greer snorted as she worked. "And how long before they ban me from *that* campus?"

Lara and Jessica giggled.

"They'd hang wanted posters in all the classrooms," Lara predicted. *"Wanted: Greer Hallsey. Crime: emotional castration of the entire male student body."*

"That would be kind of awesome." Greer squirted some product in her hands and tousled Lara's hair vigorously.

"You'll be fine," Lara assured her. "Whatever happens."

"All right, done." Greer sat back and swept her products back in her case. "Take a look."

Greer had given Lara the ultimate smoky eye — layers

of charcoal and silver eye shadow ringed her blue eyes, making them look huge. The rest of her face was pale, including her lips, which emphasized her dramatic eyes even more. Wild, piecey hair gave her a cool, androgynous look. It was straight out of *Vogue*.

Jessica was impressed. "You look incredible. Your eyes are like neon."

Lara grabbed her camera out of her bag. "I need to record this for posterity."

"Get all of us," Jessica proposed eagerly. The three girls pressed their heads together as closely as possible, smiling at the camera that Lara held at arm's length. She called out different expressions ("Goofy!" "Scary!" "Drunk!") as she took shot after shot.

"Now give me sexy, girls!" Lara yelled.

Jessica pouted, Greer half closed her eyes in a kiss, and Lara winked seductively. Laughing, Jessica grabbed the camera to look at the picture. It had managed to capture everything that her cousins turned out to be — fun, crazy . . . perfect.

Lara watched surreptitiously from behind the salad bar as Drew waved good-bye to Kate and Zoe. Now that her and Drew's fun banter had disintegrated into polite-yet-distant monosyllables, work had become the definition of awkward. She needed to talk to Zoe, but not with him around. And her newfound bonding with her cousins had given Lara a fresh appreciation for the notion of sisterhood. She cornered her friend at the soda fountain.

"Zoe, can I talk to you?"

Zoe turned, the rag in her hand stained orange from wiping up a Fanta spill. "What about?"

"The other day, in the pantry. I think you might have gotten the wrong idea."

Zoe raised a perfectly arched eyebrow. "What was the right idea?"

Lara took a deep breath. "I fell off the ladder when we were doing inventory, and Drew caught me. That's when you walked in." It wasn't exactly a lie, but Lara had told too many half-truths to feel particularly good about it.

"You fell?" Zoe asked skeptically, setting the rag on the counter so she could cross her arms.

Lara nodded. "It's true, I'm not the most graceful person in the world."

Zoe still seemed suspicious. "It looked like you guys were kissing."

"Maybe you saw our heads bang together when we fell," Lara offered, feigning confusion. "It hurt for like two days afterward." She rubbed an imaginary bump on her temple for good measure.

Zoe laughed. "You guys had the guiltiest looks on your faces."

Lara forced a chuckle. "Well, I *did* dent at least one industrial-size jar of mayo. I knew Richard would be pissed."

"'Don't drop anything,'" Zoe intoned in a familiar Australian surfer accent.

"Exactly." *She was buying it.* Lara nearly hugged her friend out of relief.

"Well, in that case . . . has Drew ever said anything about me?" Zoe asked shyly. She handed Lara a tray of refilled salt and pepper shakers to replace the empty ones on a few of the nearby tables.

"Said anything?" she repeated, slowly swapping the anchor-shaped shakers at a round four-top.

"Yeah, you know. About me." Zoe blushed. "I think he's really cute."

Lara felt her stomach plummet. She didn't know what to say. It was great that Zoe believed her lame lie, but she wasn't quite ready to pimp out her stepcousin/ex-whatever just yet. "We don't really talk much at home."

"Oh." Zoe looked disappointed. She fiddled with her order pad in her apron pocket. "Well, do you think you could? See if he might be interested?"

"Um, sure." Lara needed this conversation to be over. Now.

Zoe grabbed her arm. "I have the best idea. Remember James?"

Lara gulped and rested her tray on her hip. "Uh, yeah."

"He's been bugging me about you, and I told him we'd all go out again. He's kind of shy," Zoe explained hurriedly. "But this would be perfect!"

Puzzled, Lara asked, "What would be perfect?"

"You and James, me and Drew. Like a double date!"

Lara didn't think a worse idea had ever existed. "I don't think so, Zoe."

Zoe's face fell. "Why?"

"Uh — " Lara frantically groped for a plausible reason, but came up empty. God, she *really* sucked at this! "I'm not sure what Drew would say."

"Don't worry about it," Zoe said brightly. "If you and James are coming, then I'll ask him myself. It'll be like we're all just hanging out."

Lara gave up. She couldn't get out of this — Zoe was obviously on a mission to cause Lara intense pain. "Okay."

"Awesome!" Zoe exulted. "I'll set it up. It'll be so much fun!"

"Fun," Lara agreed dully. Zoe didn't seem to pick up on her lack of euphoria. She skipped off to attend to her neglected tables, her happy smile softening the annoyed diners. Lara approached her new customer lifelessly, but jerked in surprise when she recognized him.

"James?"

"Hey," he said cheerfully. "I've been meaning to visit you guys."

Lara summoned a smile. "Oh, that's really sweet of you."

"James!" Zoe appeared at Lara's side. "Finally!"

He shook his head. "I know, I know. But look, I made it." He waved the menu. "Which of you lovely ladies is my waitress?"

Zoe nudged Lara forward. "Lara will be your server tonight," she said mischievously. "I'm so glad you came. We need to chat." She turned to Lara. "Why don't you get him an iced tea?" she asked with a wink.

Lara moved away robotically. James was cute and perfectly nice, but when she looked at him she just didn't feel that epic *want*. Which was what she felt for Drew.

But she'd meant it when she told Drew it was over. The closer she got to Greer and Jessica, the more she realized how much her secret would hurt her new family. As amazing as their brief romance had been, there were too many lies weighing it down. And she wouldn't let herself mope about it anymore. She glanced back at the table where Zoe and James were laughing. *The best way to get over a guy is to find a new one,* she decided. And there was no time like the present.

She quickly poured the iced tea and threw a few lemon wedges in the glass. Then she brought it over to James's table and set it down with a smile.

"Are you free Friday?" Zoe asked her excitedly.

"Sure!" Lara said brightly.

"Great. I'll ask Drew tomorrow." Zoe grinned and walked away, a little too quickly.

Lara leaned on the chair opposite James, determined to make an effort. "How's lifeguarding?"

He perked up. "Awesome. We judged a contest last night."

Perplexed, Lara asked, "A swimming contest?"

"The Miss Pebble Beach pageant. They asked the lifeguards to be guest judges."

Good God. "That sounds fun," she managed to say.

"Wait till I tell you about the swimsuit competition. . . ."

"I'm all ears," Lara sighed, surreptitiously looking at her watch. It was going to be a long night.

21

Greer tapped her manicured nails on the steering wheel, lost in thought. She didn't know what to expect from her upcoming lesson. Brady hadn't called or texted after the bonfire. Officially dating or not, you didn't just *ditch* a person when your ex suddenly reappeared.

Slamming the car door, Greer stalked around the building directly to the dock. She wanted to avoid any innocent bystanders — this was between her and Brady. As she came in view of the bay, she saw a distant figure waiting by the boats. By the time she reached the dock, Greer's scowl had transformed into a disarming smile.

"Hi there," she said smoothly.

"Hi. I'm Kaitlyn Howard," the girl announced with a smirk. She wore a Stewart polo and a high ponytail. "I'll be your instructor today. Brady told me all about your . . . *progress.* Sounds like you're doing well for a beginner."

Progress? Greer folded her arms across her chest. "Where's Brady?"

"Brady couldn't make it today, so Ellen and Gerald asked me to help," Kaitlyn replied importantly. "Don't worry, I'll take *good* care of you."

"I don't doubt it," Greer muttered.

Just then, Mrs. Stewart came out of the back door and walked over to them. "Greer, dear, I hope you don't mind the last-minute change." She smiled and put a hand on Kaitlyn's shoulder. "Kaitlyn is an excellent instructor — she's practically part of our family. You're in great hands."

Lucky me.

After Mrs. Stewart went back into the clubhouse, Kaitlyn stepped onto a bigger boat than Greer usually sailed. "Well?" she asked impatiently. "Come on."

With an inward sigh, Greer joined Kaitlyn on board. She couldn't believe that instead of Brady, here was Ex-zilla, who obviously knew there was something between Greer and Brady.

As the girls sailed out and the wind blew their hair back, Kaitlyn reveled in her authority, issuing commands that Greer didn't understand and gleefully criticizing every mistake. Knowing that Kaitlyn would report back to the

Stewarts at the end of the lesson, Greer gritted her teeth and did the best she could.

Kaitlyn barked out one directive after another, forcing Greer to run, lift, push, and pull in quick succession. When she had the boat smoothly cutting through the water, she plunked down on the deck to catch her breath.

"Coil that rope," Kaitlyn ordered sharply.

Greer got up and began coiling. "So, you and Brady used to date?" she asked flat out.

"Brady and I are complicated," Kaitlyn replied. "You wouldn't understand."

"That's probably true," Greer cooed sympathetically. "Brady and *I* are so nice and simple."

Kaitlyn suddenly pulled the jib sheet out of the cleat, slowing the boat by turning it across the wind. Greer had taken enough lessons to know that you didn't just stop a boat spontaneously like that, unless something was wrong. She stood anxiously, wanting to know but not wanting to ask.

Finally, Kaitlyn turned to her, her hostility replaced by concern. "I need you to check the transom," she said urgently.

"What? Why?" Brady had never asked her to do that.

"I think there's something wrong with the rudder, but I have to stay up here and hold the boat still. You need to go down and look."

"In the water?" Greer shook her head. "I have no idea what a rudder is supposed to look like."

"Do you really want to be stuck here together until someone happens to come by?"

Greer sighed in resignation. She bent down to unlace her gold Pumas, but a sudden hard shove sent her tumbling over the edge of the boat. She plunged into the ocean, taking in a mouthful of salty water. After the shock from the cold had passed, she kicked instinctively for the surface. When she broke through, Kaitlyn was hoisting the jib with a smile. As soon as she tied it in place, the wind snapped the sail and propelled the boat forward and away.

Oh. My. God!

Greer treaded water, lost in disbelief, indignation, and a tiny iota of grudging respect. The girl had balls. Unfortunately, she very likely also had the nerve to leave Greer out here forever. Greer scanned the water, judging the distance to the club to be about a half mile. No boaters or Jet Skiers around. *Well, I'll just have to rescue myself, then.*

Not one to waste time bemoaning her fate, Greer mournfully abandoned her Pumas to reduce the drag and kicked into a strong crawl toward the shore. It was longer than she'd ever swum before, but outrage kept her going. After what seemed like forever, Greer finally felt the rocky bottom under her tired feet. Every last person on the beach stared as she emerged from the waves, shaking the droplets out of her long, dark hair. Her soaking wet top and shorts clung to every curve of her body, water streaming onto the sand as she stood and tried to catch her breath.

She thought she'd spotted Brady running to meet her, but he had inexplicably frozen in place, watching her with his mouth slightly agape. When she met his eyes, he quickly snapped out of his daze and ran forward with a towel.

He wrapped her in the huge towel and looked into her face. "Are you okay?"

"I'm fine." She spotted Kaitlyn standing alone on the dock. "I think I need to take off these wet clothes, though," she suggested with a cough.

Brady swung her up easily into his arms and walked toward the dock. He apologized earnestly, blaming himself for not being there. Greer was only half listening. She felt as light as a feather in his strong, muscled arms.

"And I'm not sure if Kaitlyn mentioned this, but she's my ex-girlfriend," Brady said, looking uncomfortable. "It didn't end well. But my parents asked her to help out while I practice for the regatta at the end of the month."

Greer nestled against his shoulder. "I figured there was a reason she pushed me off the boat."

"Unbelievable," Brady shook his head. "She said you jumped off and refused to get back in."

As they reached the dock, Brady set his jaw and looked straight ahead. Kaitlyn reached out and touched his elbow when they passed her. "Brady, let me explain."

He stopped. "Don't bother," he informed her coldly.

Kaitlyn stumbled back, and he continued up the dock. Greer looked back and saw the murderous look on Kaitlyn's freckled face. Greer returned it with a smile and a wink. With Brady's arms holding her tightly against his solid chest, she could afford to be generous.

He sat her down gently on a bench inside the club. "Look, my parents aren't here right now, but I can take you to the hospital." His face was clouded with concern.

Greer shook her head. "I'm fine, really. I'm just a little cold. And tired. And really wet."

"Right, let me get you some clothes." He returned quickly with a pair of his mother's shorts and a pink Stewart Yacht Club T-shirt. "Compliments of the house," he joked halfheartedly.

She stripped off her shorts and tank, deliberately letting Brady get another eyeful of her bikini before pulling the dry clothes on.

"Thanks for the clothes," she began, gathering her wet things into a towel and sitting back down on the bench. "And whatever's going on with you and Kaitlyn is none of my business —"

"I'm so sorry you got dragged into this, Greer."

She shrugged off his apology. "There's nothing to be sorry about. I know you and I are just getting to know each other, but . . ."

He nodded, saying nothing.

She went on honestly. "I just hope everything works out the way you want it to. It's always complicated with exes." She smiled. "And if you ever just want to talk, I'm actually a pretty good listener."

Brady looked at her searchingly, like he was looking at someone he didn't entirely understand. "Thanks, Greer. I really appreciate that."

She stood to leave, but he held her back. "I have to apologize for the other night, at the bonfire," he said quietly but firmly. "I shouldn't have left you. I definitely shouldn't have left you the way I did. It was the first time I'd seen her since — well, since we broke up. I had a lot I needed to say. But I was a jerk to you, and I'm sorry."

When she met his eyes, all of the pain that she'd decided to ignore at the bonfire threatened to bubble up again. Not knowing what to say, she just nodded.

And as Greer walked out to her car, she sent mental thanks to Kaitlyn. There was nothing like a little perspective to help a guy make up his mind.

22

lunch b4 lax? beach 30min

Jessica read Connor's text again, puzzled. They'd settled into a daily routine with lacrosse training, but lunch was something new. She shrugged and started to respond, glad to have the chance to work on her tan some more. Suddenly, she had a brilliant idea. Excitedly, she erased her simple "sure" and typed:

ok. bring liam = beach party!

She hit SEND and grinned. She could show off her haute new look and remind him about the Jet Ski lesson he'd promised. Jessica carefully applied her makeup as Greer had shown her, though she impulsively switched to a sexy red lipstick. She checked her watch. *Game time.* She changed into a bikini and put on Greer's denim miniskirt and red Marc Jacobs tank top.

Jessica made her way to the place where Liam and Connor had taken her the day they all met. She spotted Connor sitting on the sand, leaning against a cooler with his shirt off, but without his brother. He stood up quickly when he saw her, but he frowned deeply as she got closer. She suddenly felt very self-conscious about her very exposed legs.

"What are you wearing?" he blurted, looking mildly horrified. Suddenly, she was glad that Liam wasn't there.

"Um, I thought we were having lunch," she sort of explained.

"Yeah," he agreed, still looking confused. "But what about training? You can't practice in . . . that." He looked at her legs quickly, then averted his eyes.

She was getting irritated. *What was the big deal?* "Let's skip the workout today. We can train tomorrow."

Connor shook his head and eyed her strangely. "I don't get it," he muttered.

Jessica changed the subject, feeling intensely awkward just standing there staring at each other. "So what's the occasion?" she asked, pointing at the cooler.

"No occasion," he said, finally smiling. "Just thought

we could try doing something besides attacking each other with sticks for a change."

"Nice," she agreed, digging her big toe into the sand. She summoned all the nonchalance she was capable of as she looked out at the glittery water. "So, where's Liam? Didn't you ask him to come?"

Connor stared down at the sand for a moment. Then, as he bent down to pick up the cooler, he looked her squarely in the eyes. "Tell you what," he said quietly. "Why don't you go find him and have a nice lunch together." He thrust the cooler into her hands and walked away toward the pier.

Jessica felt a surge of hurt and surprise. She knelt down on the hot sand and opened the cooler. Inside was the perfect picnic: two turkey sandwiches, Doritos, Gatorade, and Hostess snack-size apple pies, which she had once confessed to Connor were her favorite things ever.

She bit her lip. Connor had obviously put some thought into this. She sat and waited, hoping he'd come back so she could apologize. She traced circles in the golden sand with her finger, trying to think of what she'd say to him.

"This is a nice surprise."

She looked up, startled. Liam stood over her, holding on to a surfboard. He smiled. "Catching some sun?"

She nodded and stood up, glad to put her outfit to use after all. "I was just thinking about what to do today," she said offhandedly, putting a hand on her hip and raising her eyebrows. Still, she couldn't shake the guilt she felt over Connor. Why had he gotten so upset?

Liam's eyes traveled down her legs. "Do you surf?"

"No, but I'd love to learn," she hinted with a smile.

He nodded his head toward the ocean. "Well, come on. You can use my board."

Jessica joyfully stripped off the magic outfit and followed Liam into the water. She quickly discovered that her bodysurfing skills were entirely useless for actual surfing — standing on a moving piece of wet plastic was a hundred times harder than lying on it. But Liam was a patient teacher. He helped her paddle out and get the feel of standing on the board. He told her when to jump off to avoid getting tumbled.

When she finally managed to keep her balance on a baby wave, Liam clapped and gave a piercing whistle. Jessica blushed happily as she paddled toward him.

"You're a natural," he told her, steadying the board. "Pretty soon, you'll be kicking my butt at competitions like you kick my brother's butt at lax."

She laughed as she slid off, ignoring the pang she felt at the mention of Connor. "It'll be sweet revenge for beating me at Wii tennis."

They walked back to Jessica's pile of clothes. "Want something to eat?" she offered.

He shook his head. "I've gotta practice. This was fun," he added with a grin.

"Thanks for the lesson," she replied, hoping he would ask her out. *Please please please.*

"All right, see ya." Liam turned and jogged back down to the water, leaving her a little surprised and a *lot* disappointed.

Unhappily, she carried her clothes and the cooler to her backyard. She fell into the hammock with the Doritos, staring up at the cloudless blue sky, pondering the many mysteries of boys.

Spotting her from the deck, Drew ran across the yard and jumped on her, nearly spilling them both on the ground. "Hey, sis! What's happening, stranger?"

"Not much," she said morosely, passing him the bag. "You?"

He grunted in reply.

"I have a question for you."

He settled more comfortably into the hammock. "Shoot."

Jessica felt awkward asking her brother, but there was a serious lack of male perspective available to her. "If you liked a girl, wouldn't you try to hang out with her as much as possible?"

Drew digested the question. "Within reason, but I couldn't just abandon the rest of my life," he answered thoughtfully. "I'd hope she'd be the kind of girl who understands that I still have work or school or family stuff."

Jessica exhaled. She hadn't even realized she was holding her breath. She tossed her brother the Doritos and hopped out of the hammock, giving it a dangerous push before she trotted up to the house.

"Really?" he called after her, struggling to control the swinging net. "I impart my wisdom and you try to kill me?"

"Yup. Payback for years of wedgies," Jessica shouted over her shoulder and she made her way up to the door.

Leave it to her brother to make it all seem simple. Liam *had* to like her. The flirting and the way he looked at her . . . But he had a surf competition coming up and the carpentry work and whatever else. She just needed some patience. She climbed the stairs to her room, holding the borrowed clothes tightly to her chest. She'd wait all summer if she had to. Although she really hoped she wouldn't have to.

23

Lara was in a special circle of hell, the one reserved for the really evil people who kicked puppies or spread computer viruses on purpose. She stirred her coffee listlessly as she offered canned answers to James's questions about every aspect of her life. Work. School. Chicago. Her mother. Her dead parakeet.

She'd started the date optimistically, remembering her vow to move on with her life. But with Zoe and Drew having their own date less than two feet away, optimism was proving hard to maintain. And as the night progressed, Lara's glaring incompatibility with James made the minutes all the more difficult to endure.

"What's your school mascot?" James inquired.

Wow. Just, wow.

"Um, I honestly don't know." Lara drummed her spoon on the table. Zoe and Drew sat opposite them, talking animatedly about something. Probably not school mascots.

"What do you think, Lara?" Suddenly, Zoe looked at her expectantly. The light from the paper lantern swinging above their heads flickered off of her glossy curls. She looked annoyingly beautiful.

"Think about what?" Lara was actually relieved to talk to the girl who was on a date with the boy she herself had fallen for. A definite sign of misery.

Drew spoke up. "I was saying that band names suck these days, and Zoe disagrees."

Lara had been careful not to direct too much of her conversation at Drew tonight, but it felt good to fall back into their easy rapport. "I don't know," she said thoughtfully. "Maybe all the good ones are taken."

Drew scoffed. "Pick any literary reference or historical figure and you've got yourself an interesting band name," he pointed out. "I'm just saying, bands are getting really lazy. The Hives. The Veronicas. The Holloways. What happened to good names like Ned's Atomic Dustbin and Guns N' Roses?" He took a vengeful bite of his fish taco.

God, she'd missed his opinionated rants — usually misguided, but always earnest. "But the names mean something to the bands, even if you don't get it. Where's your faith in musicians?"

He smirked. "It was crushed by the Jonas Brothers."

Lara laughed, then suddenly noticed that Zoe and James had started talking to each other. Feeling guilty, she tried joining in, but they were complaining about something at school.

Lara and Drew fell silent, but she glanced at him from under her lashes. His dark hair had grown even floppier as the summer progressed. A couple days worth of stubble gave him an irresistible just-rolled-out-of-bed look that made Lara want to grab his face and kiss him right in front of Zoe and James.

Her fantasy was interrupted by the arrival of the bill, which the boys swiftly paid.

"So how about we go out to the beach?" James offered a hand to help Lara out of the booth. She stood, and he put his arm around her, causing her to stiffen involuntarily.

"Oh, shoot. I'd love to, but I promised my mom I'd get back early tonight," she invented. "Uh, I have to help her with some freelance project she's working on."

Zoe cast her a disbelieving look. "You have to do this *tonight*?"

Lara shrugged. "She's paying for half my car." She tried to look as disappointed as possible, considering she was actually counting the seconds until this whole evening would end.

"I'll walk you home," James offered, his voice hopeful.

Lara forced herself to smile. The last thing she wanted was alone time with James. On the beach. In the dark.

"We could hang out on the beach," Drew told Zoe. Lara's heart lurched. Okay, the last, *last* thing she wanted was for Drew and Zoe to have alone time. She felt sick as she thought about what happened alone, on beaches, in the dark.

Not making eye contact with either of them, she turned toward home. "Have a good night, guys," she said quickly. James returned his arm to her shoulders again and steered her off the wooden platform onto the beach.

They got about fifty yards before she turned to him, unable to stand it any longer. "Look, James, I'd really like to walk the rest of the way alone. I'm sorry." She shrugged his arm off.

"What's wrong?" He looked confused.

"Me," she told him, and turned away. "I'm really sorry," she offered again. It sounded as lame as she felt.

She trudged home through the dark night. The only sounds were her feet scuffling along and the chirping of crickets in the tall beach grass.

Until she got within earshot of her house.

Standing on the deck were her mother and stepfather, having a major fight.

"That is *not* what I said, and you know it!" Her mother's voice rose an octave higher with each outraged word.

"All I know is that it's impossible to have a discussion with you right now," Mike fired back. "You're completely irrational."

Lara cringed. *Wrong thing to say, buddy.*

"Don't patronize me!" her mother shouted. "How dare you?"

Lara fled upstairs to her room. She sat on her bed and stared bleakly at her quilt. Mike was number five. Lara had gotten used to the parade of men that her mother had married, but she'd hoped this one would stick. And now it looked like this one wasn't even going to last a year. Tears blurred the bright patchwork outlines on the bed, and Lara's body shook with silent sobbing.

Greer and Jessica walked in quietly, and Lara wondered if they heard the argument. Her cousins sat next to her, resting their hands on her quivering shoulders.

"This summer isn't exactly what I expected," Lara finally admitted.

The other girls remained silent, but Lara was comforted just by their presence. They had so recently been strangers, and now they really felt like cousins, an idea she was still getting used to. Tonight, for the first time in her life, she was scared of losing a family.

Part of her wished Drew was there to soothe her with his clear green eyes, but to her surprise, a larger part of her was glad he wasn't. It was nice to have it be just the summer girls.

24

Greer was looking forward to her next sailing lesson. They obviously wouldn't stick her with Kaitlyn, so chances were that she'd never have to deal with her again.

But as she approached the dock, Greer's spirits sank. Brady was waiting for her. With Kaitlyn standing unnecessarily close.

"Hi, Greer," a voice chirped beside her.

Greer glanced down. "Hey, Clara," she replied, pleased to see the younger girl. "I like your French braid. Very pretty."

"Thank you," Clara said automatically, practically bouncing as she kept pace with Greer's long strides down the grass. "Kaitlyn did it. She's the only one who can besides Mom."

"That's nice," Greer lied, no longer all that thrilled with her twelve-year-old sidekick.

"Are you going to the regatta next weekend?"

"I think so." Greer couldn't even try to match Clara's energy. "Your brother mentioned it. Are you racing?"

Clara's face clouded over. "I only do the juniors." She perked up. "Next year, though, I'll be allowed to crew."

"That's great." The girl's enthusiasm would've been infectious if every step Greer took didn't bring her closer to the dreaded ex waiting on the dock.

"Yeah, especially if I can help *Princess Kaitlyn* win again!"

Greer almost tripped. "Princess Kaitlyn?"

"It's Kaitlyn's family's boat," Clara explained. "Isn't it a pretty name? Brady crews every year, and next year she said I could, too! Want to see a picture of the trophy?"

Good Lord. "Maybe later, Clara. I have to start my lesson now."

"Okay. Bye!" Clara danced across the lawn and into the clubhouse. Greer watched her for a moment, envying her carefree spirit. Then she steeled herself to join Brady and Kaitlyn.

"Good morning," she said cheerfully. Kaitlyn smirked but said nothing.

Brady looked confused at her unexpected reaction. "Um, Kaitlyn is going to help out today. She feels really bad about what happened and wanted to come." He glanced at his ex, clearly thinking this was a bad idea. Greer had to hand it to the girl. She knew how to get what she wanted.

Kaitlyn spoke up. "I'm really sorry about the other day. How about we start over?" She fixed her brown eyes on Greer, daring her to complain.

"Of course," Greer said graciously. "I'm not really up for swimming today, though," she warned with an overly friendly smile. "My watch isn't waterproof."

Brady helped them both onto the boat. As the lesson began, Kaitlyn stayed on the sidelines and kept out of Greer's way while Brady gave orders. When they were out on the water, Brady called for a break.

"I hope the weather holds out for the regatta," Kaitlyn commented, shading her eyes from the sun.

Brady looked up at the sails. "Well, the wind has a week to pick up. We can always use a little push."

Kaitlyn grinned broadly. "The boat's in awesome shape, so I think we have a good chance again this year." She rubbed her hands together excitedly.

Brady's eyes sparkled. "Oh, man, two in a row would be wicked."

Greer looked out to the sea disconsolately. Brady had been unusually quiet throughout the lesson, blandly confirming she'd done things correctly. But at Kaitlyn's mention of the regatta, he suddenly got chatty.

"Remember last year during training, when the boom hit you in the face?" Kaitlyn laughed, leaning against the mast.

Brady grinned sheepishly. "That hurt like crazy."

"And then your ice pack gave you frostbite!" Kaitlyn glanced at Greer. The girls locked eyes momentarily. Clearly, Kaitlyn knew what she was doing.

"Freezer burn," he corrected.

Greer rolled her eyes. She had absolutely nothing to add. So she waited for a lull in racing chatter, then sighed.

"You know what I could really go for right now?" she asked to no one in particular. "A funnel cake. With lots and lots of powdered sugar." She gave Brady a conspiratorial smile.

He grinned slowly, hopefully remembering what happened after the last funnel cake they'd shared. "We should go get one after the lesson."

Greer held his gaze. "I'd love that," she purred. Ask a guy to choose between sailing and making out with a hot girl, and there was no contest. She glanced at Kaitlyn out of the corner of her eye. Her freckly face was screwed up in a frustrated grimace. She stood up purposefully when she caught Greer's triumphant smile.

"We should head back," Kaitlyn announced. "Greer, the wind's picking up. What do you know about reefing?"

Caught off guard, Greer stammered, "Um, it means —"

"You can't afford to think slow when you're sailing," Kaitlyn said crisply.

Stunned by the unfairness of the attack, Greer kept quiet. Kaitlyn pressed her advantage. "Can you tell us two methods of reefing that we use at Stewart?"

Greer shook her head. She looked to Brady for confirmation that she definitely hadn't been taught this stuff, but he was watching Kaitlyn with a bemused expression. After so many lessons, she was mortified by how easily Kaitlyn made her look stupid. Plus, she hadn't missed all the "we's" that Kaitlyn was throwing around.

Before Kaitlyn could question her again, Greer pointed beyond the starboard side. "Isn't that where you stranded me? It's so much farther away from shore than I thought."

Bingo. Kaitlyn pursed her lips and busied herself with some lines, while Brady followed Greer's pointing and whistled.

"That's pretty far," Brady agreed. "How'd a city girl like you learn how to swim?"

"Nursery school at the Y, summers at the beach," she recalled. "I've always loved the water."

"I know the feeling." He smiled at her. "Would you mind moving?"

Greer was used to this order. She switched to the port side, and Brady steered the boat toward the club. Unfortunately, this put the mast between her and Brady, ending their conversation. Kaitlyn took the opportunity to challenge Greer on mooring procedures, and again Greer was at a loss. Brady silently brought the boat home, and Greer picked up the dock line.

"Sit down," Kaitlyn snapped at her. She grabbed the line out of Greer's hand. "I'll handle it. You barely know what a boat is."

Loathing every freckle on her co-teacher's face, Greer sat stonily still. It was one thing to be stranded at sea by this wench, but it was another thing to be insulted by her right in front of Brady. He hadn't stood up for her *once*. The moment the boat docked, she jumped out and turned for the clubhouse.

Brady called after her, "Aren't we going for that funnel cake?"

She paused and looked back. He was watching her, but Kaitlyn was tugging on his sleeve, reminding him about training. Greer shook her head slightly and walked away.

25

*A little red Mini Cooper, or maybe a VW convertible bug . . .
Drew in the passenger seat, laughing as we speed down the
Pacific Coast Highway with the top down . . .*

Lara's daydream played out like an old-school movie as
she idled over the menu at the Okay Café. She'd just finished a shift at Ahoy and desperately needed something
with a high chocolate content.

When the waitress came, Lara ordered a brownie à la
mode. From Zoe's post-date gushing to surviving working
with Drew on a daily basis, she deserved a reward for her
pain and suffering. Plus, her mother had been sulking like a
child since the fight Lara had overheard the other night.

She had just popped the maraschino cherry in her
mouth when a voice startled her.

"Mind if I join you?"

She looked up, the cherry's stem poking out between her lips. Greer stood next to her, looking fabulous in all white.

Lara pulled out the stem. "What are you doing here?" she asked curiously.

Greer scowled, dropping into the cozy booth. "I just had my sailing lesson."

"No love on the high seas?" Lara guessed, twirling her spoon above the little bit of chocolate heaven on the table.

Greer launched into a play-by-play of Kaitlyn's latest assault.

"I'm getting the suspicion that this girl might not like you very much," Lara observed. "What about Brady?"

Greer sighed and fiddled with the decorative miniature jukebox on the table. "We'll just see what happens at the regatta, I guess. He'll be racing her boat, though."

Lara took a bite of her brownie. "Sounds like a sticky situation. But if anyone can handle it, you can."

Greer shook her head ruefully. "I'm not sure what I can handle anymore. Everything's weird this summer."

That's an understatement. "Can I tell you something?" Lara was suddenly desperate to confide in someone and Greer seemed like the best candidate.

"Sure."

How to begin? "I've been sort of seeing someone I shouldn't be," Lara started hesitantly, her pulse picking up.

"That James guy?"

"Um, no," Lara admitted slowly. "He was sort of a decoy . . . for Jessica."

Greer looked puzzled. "What are you talking about?"

Lara took a deep breath. *Here goes.* "It's Drew," she blurted. *Oh, God.*

She peeked at Greer. Greer's hands were frozen in front of her face, mid-manicure check. Her mouth opened and closed twice, but no sound emerged.

Finally, she spoke. "Drew Tuttle?"

Lara managed to nod.

"Lara . . . that's — how's that going to work?"

Lara groaned. "I know it's totally impossible — and so does he. But the feelings just won't go away. I've never liked anyone this much. And working together — we see each other so often. It's just . . . hard."

Another pause.

Greer contemplated the ceiling for a moment. "Well, your mom just married Uncle Mike, like, yesterday . . ." Greer trailed off, looking Lara in the eye. "I guess I can kinda see you guys together."

Lara felt a weight lift off her shoulders. "But Jessica . . ."

"I wouldn't tell her," Greer said quickly, placing her hands on the tabletop. "I'm pretty sure she'd flip out."

"Right, okay." Lara would rather not keep secrets, but she doubted anything would happen between her and Drew again. So what was the point of opening an unnecessary wound? She sighed.

"So . . . Drew, huh?" Greer looked at her speculatively. "Is it still going on, or . . . ?"

"Not at the moment." There was so much Lara wasn't saying — how she wanted to do the right thing and not mess up the family. But how could she explain her fear of losing a family she so recently gained to Greer? Greer had been born into the Tuttles, after all. Lara was still on probation. "Anyway, he might be dating Zoe."

"I wouldn't worry about the stepcousin thing if that's what's stopping you," Greer advised.

"Yeah, especially since my mom's probably already called her divorce attorney," Lara said glumly. "They're BFFs at this point."

Greer's face went blank. Lara instantly regretted what she said. "I'm sorry, Greer."

"There's nothing to be sorry about." She got up. "I think it's time for some retail therapy. Want to come?"

"I'm undergoing chocolate therapy right now, but thanks."

"Suit yourself." Greer shugged her white Poloed

shoulders. "But personally, I'm going to go buy a new suit. Swimsuit," she clarified her own pun with a grin.

Lara rolled her eyes and waved good-bye dejectedly.

Ever since her mother's fight with Uncle Mike, Lara had just been waiting for the other shoe to drop. She hadn't seen her mom and Mike much since the fight, but she was familiar with the dreaded signs. So there was every chance that Drew wouldn't be her stepcousin anymore by the end of the summer.

But neither would Greer and Jessica.

Lara wasn't sure which option she preferred. Not that it would be up to her. Not that it ever was.

26

"We can't all wear the same color!" Greer said, exasperated. "How cheesy is that?"

"Oh, I don't know," Lara said contrarily. "I think we'd look cute, like triplets."

Jessica looked at her cousins, then down at herself. "I'm going with Greer on this one," she decided.

Lara rolled her eyes — a habit that she'd picked up from Greer, Jessica thought — and pulled off her blue T-shirt. Without looking, she reached into her dresser drawer and put on a black tank printed with the Rolling Stones tongue. She looked at the other girls expectantly. "Shall we?"

Jessica went to the mirror again and looked at herself critically. She envied Lara's carefree style. She had borrowed Greer's Alice + Olivia electric-blue sundress. The rich silk made her tanned skin glow, but she felt a little over-dressed. "Are you sure this isn't too much?" she asked again, nervously.

Greer emitted a strangled noise. Lara quickly spoke up. "You look fantastic, Jess. Magnificent. Gorgeous. Every word for 'great' in the English language."

Jessica giggled. "I'm sorry to be such a pain. I just need to look good today."

"He'll burst a vein when he sees you," Lara predicted, running a dollop of pomade through her short hair.

"You look fabulous, Jessi," Greer confirmed. "Now can we go?"

Jessica took one last peek at herself. "Showtime."

The cousins walked down to the beach, where a large crowd had already formed to watch the regatta. Large white tents were set up all along the sand. The race wasn't due to start for an hour, but Greer had wanted to go early. As they wandered among the sailing enthusiasts, Jessica couldn't help but be caught up in the competitive excitement, even though she didn't know anything about boats. This was what she loved most about being an athlete. The anticipation, the adrenaline rush, the energy from the competitors and the spectators was exhilarating.

She spotted Connor nearby, hanging out with a group of friends. He hadn't called or come by in the two weeks since their fight. She'd texted, but he hadn't replied. She'd really missed their training sessions. She waved at him, smiling, but he looked away quickly. Stung, she followed her cousins farther down the beach.

They found a spot with an unobstructed view of the water and set down the cooler they'd brought, which Greer had liberally stocked with wine and beer.

"Are you nervous for Brady?" Jessica asked Greer as Lara took pictures of the boats bobbing in the water.

"No, he's a great sailor, and his crew won last year," Greer replied with a hint of pride. "I just wish he wasn't on Hate-lyn's boat."

"He'll be done in a few hours," Lara pointed out, and Greer smiled grimly.

As if on cue, an air horn blasted through the buzzing crowd. Greer set her Solo cup down and stood, smoothing the wrinkles from her long, batik-printed dress. "Time for a stroll."

Lara hopped up, too. "It's time I met this young man," she explained.

Jessica waved them off, then turned to the ocean. She leaned back on her elbows, watching white caps form a little ways offshore. She loved this time of day, with the sun high, daubing each ocean wave with glitter. She watched a group of surfers with interest, admiring their grace on the waves. As she looked closer, she recognized Liam's tousled hair. He looked amazing and strong on his board.

He surfed until the lifeguards whistled a final warning in anticipation of the race. He emerged from the surf not far from where she sat, and she energetically waved. Saying something to his friends, he jogged toward her with a smile. She watched him approach like a sun god, his chest brown and sinewy, his light eyes glowing underneath damp hair.

"Hey, you," he said as he reached her. "All alone again?"

"My cousins are around here somewhere," she explained, her heart beating faster. "Want a beer?"

He jammed his board into the sand and accepted a bottle with a smile, sitting next to her in the sand.

"Hey, you had a competition last week, right? How'd it go?" Jessica asked.

He grinned. "Third place."

"That's awesome!" Jessica was impressed. Even after just one lesson, she knew how much work it took to surf at his level. It turned out that they had something in common after all.

"Thanks," he said, looking slightly embarrassed. "It's not a big deal."

"When's the next one?" she asked, hoping for a far-off date so he'd have lots of time to devote to her. Once she got him to admit how much he liked her, of course.

He tipped the rest of the beer into his mouth. "Not sure, maybe next month." He glanced at his watch. "I have to find my parents. We always watch the race together." He paused and looked at her awkwardly. "Want to come?"

Jessica was thrilled, but regretfully shook her head. *Why did he have to ask so last minute?* "I should stay in case Greer and Lara come back."

He shrugged. "Cool. You're coming to the after party, right?"

"I think so."

"Excellent. I'll see you tonight, then." He smiled as he grabbed his board.

Jessica watched as he picked his way between the dense spread of blankets. The starting horn sounded, and she stood to watch the race begin. The white boats looked like a postcard against the crisp blue sky. The crowd cheered as the boats moved out into the ocean, and Jessica clapped her hands along with them. As perfect as this scene was, she couldn't wait for it to be over. Tonight couldn't come fast enough.

27

Greer found Brady waiting for her in the corner of the staging tent, as promised. When he spotted her through the crowd, his face lit up.

She left Lara at the food table and walked over. She stretched to kiss his cheek. "That's for good luck, sailor."

He chuckled. "I'll take another one, then." He offered her the other side of his face.

She smiled. "Don't forget which side is port and which is starboard."

"Thanks." Brady's face grew serious for a moment. "Uh, I need to apologize to you about last week."

He paused, gathering his thoughts. Greer wanted to interject, but she forced herself to wait. When he looked up, she noted the sincerity in his eyes.

"I'm sorry I let her treat you like that. I should have realized what was going to happen. She can be really . . . stubborn."

Greer couldn't help snorting. Brady shook his head. "I know, that isn't exactly the right word for it. She wasn't always like this. I think our breakup's been hard on her."

"Has it been hard on you?" Greer looked at him searchingly. The crowd in the tent buzzed with prerace excitement, but she felt like she and Brady were in their own little world.

"Of course," he said quickly. But he paused thoughtfully before continuing. "I was really hurt and probably still am, a little," he said finally. "Luckily, I met you. She's just having a harder time moving on."

She smiled. That was even more satisfying than she'd imagined. "Apology accepted. But no more lessons with Kaitlyn. Period."

"I can arrange that." He laughed and squeezed her tightly. The tiny bit of lingering tension between them evaporated.

She glanced at him coyly. "Can you arrange to meet me at the after party, too?"

"Done." He held out his hand and she shook it. "I'm really glad I watched you tap that keg," he reflected. The memory of their first meeting made Greer smile.

"There could be many more perfectly poured beers in your future if you play your cards right," she told him. "But they come at a high price."

He raised an eyebrow. "Sailing lessons? That's all I've got."

"Oh, no it's not." Greer smiled mischievously.

Brady blushed, and he held her gaze. She could feel a few people looking at them and knew how good they must look together.

"Hey, cuz." Lara bumped Greer's hip with her own, a napkin full of cheese cubes in her palm.

Greer smirked. "Fancy seeing you here."

"I know! Small world." Lara turned to Brady and extended a hand. "Forgive her rudeness. I'm Lara."

Brady's blue eyes sparkled with amusement. "Brady. Of course I'll have to forgive her. She's just lucky she's so cute."

Lara eyed him appraisingly. "So you're the guy who's been torturing my dear cousin all summer, eh?" Greer shot her a look. "On the water, I mean," Lara added hastily.

"I guess you could say that," Brady said, snaking his arm around Greer's waist. "But it's only because she has so much potential." His strong hand pulled her an inch closer to him.

Lara laughed as Greer rolled her eyes. "Well, go easy on her. She's very sensitive and fragile, as I'm sure you know."

"And that's enough of that," Greer said through gritted teeth as the horn sounded.

Brady removed his arm and faced her. "Thirty minutes to the start." He squeezed her hand. "I'll see you at the party."

Greer nodded. "Kick ass out there."

He kissed her lightly, sending a tingle through her body. "Thanks." He gave Lara a friendly nod. "Good meeting you."

"A pleasure," Lara agreed as he retreated into the crowd. She looked at Greer with an eyebrow raised. "Not bad . . . not bad at all. He belongs on a Wheaties box. Or a J.Crew catalog."

"Let's go watch the race." Greer stopped her before she started picturing Brady on a Calvin Klein tighty-whities box. She glanced back as Lara led the way. Brady stood with his parents and Clara. She felt a pang as she saw them laughing together, like a picture-perfect family. Then, Greer watched as Kaitlyn joined the group, flanked by her parents. The Stewarts greeted them warmly, and Brady put an arm affectionately around his ex-girlfriend's shoulders. Greer set her shoulders back, comforting herself with the memory of Brady's words. *Take that, Kaitlyn.*

Half an hour later, the starting horn blasted, and a rush of spectators eagerly squeezed closer to the water. Greer shaded her eyes and watched the boats take off, the *Princess*

Kaitlyn somewhere among them. She clapped her hands excitedly, silently urging him to win. It would be fun to have something to celebrate tonight. More important, the sooner his boat came in, the sooner she'd be in Brady's arms, where she belonged.

28

Lara wandered aimlessly through the raucous crowds, heading in the direction of home. She knew she should find Jessica, but she couldn't muster up enough interest to sit in the hot sun and watch the race. Plus, she hadn't had a good, long stretch of quiet for a while.

She should check in on her mom, too. She'd felt guilty about avoiding her since the fight with Mike. The thought of going through the divorce process again made her temples throb.

As she unlocked the gate, she spotted Drew lying on the hammock. Considering she'd been torturing herself about what to say to him for days, she felt unusually calm crossing the yard.

For her first words, she went with her gut.

"Hi," she said, sitting on the ground in front of him. The houses looked empty. The family was down on the beach along with the rest of the town.

"Hi."

She looked at him sideways. "I've been wanting to talk to you."

Drew furrowed his brow. "Okay." His green eyes looked cloudier than she'd seen them before. Despite his reclining position, his body seemed tense.

Lara was silent for a moment. *Short and sweet,* she decided. "I want to be with you, but I don't want to turn the family upside down."

She nervously waited for a response. *He's seeing Zoe now,* she guessed, *or he's not feeling it the way I am.* Either way, she just wanted him to say something. Anything.

Finally, he spoke. "All I think about is you," he admitted gruffly. Her heart leaped. "But you always freak out when we get close to something."

She nodded solemnly. "I've been on this seesaw between liking you and not wanting things to get messy." She smiled wryly, leaning against the tree supporting the hammock. "I'm not usually so psycho, you know."

"You could've fooled me."

She kicked the hammock. "Can I finish?"

He nodded.

"My mom's headed for Divorceville. Again."

He leaned over and put a hand on her arm, looking concerned. "Are you sure?"

She shrugged. It was out of her hands. She could resent her mother, but she couldn't hold a grudge. Her lovable, irresponsible mom always had to follow her flighty little heart. "There is the one silver lining."

He chuckled. "Is that what I am? A silver lining?"

She fought a grin. "So, in conclusion, I'd like to try again. For real, this time. If you feel the same way." She paused when he didn't speak immediately. "Do you?"

In response, he got up and grabbed her waist, pulling her onto the hammock on top of him. She was surprised, but she didn't resist. Turning so that their faces were just inches apart, he tenderly stroked her short black hair. "I think I came to the same conclusion about five minutes after I saw you sitting on the deck with Jessi that first night."

She widened her eyes. "Why didn't you say anything?"

"I didn't want to have to convince you. You needed to either resolve your doubts, or not."

She digested his wisdom. It made sense.

"Of course, I thought after we made out on the beach, all your objections would naturally go away." He grinned, playing with the hair on her forehead.

She moved closer and pecked him quickly on the mouth. He grasped her face in his hands and responded with a long, lingering kiss. She felt all of her feelings — joy, excitement, infatuation, love even — rising up inside her, and for the first time, she allowed them to spill over. Their breathing became ragged as Drew's hands began roving down her body. Lara struggled to sit up in the hammock, startling him as she pulled away.

"Let's go inside," she said, smiling.

Drew ran a hand through his messy hair to compose himself. He took her hand and led her into the dark, empty house where he was staying. Holding hands, they climbed the stairs, and Lara felt nervousness blooming inside her — but as soon as they slipped into Drew's room and locked the door, she felt a fresh certainty. She'd never done this before, because she hadn't ever found a guy who was special enough. She'd never been sure. Now, she was so sure.

Drew looked a little nervous, too, Lara thought, but then he smiled and they began kissing again, even more feverishly this time. They shed their clothes, slowly and deliberately, and Lara felt beautiful in the moonlight spilling through Drew's drawn shades. As Drew laid her down gently on his bed, Lara knew that she'd made the right decision. In fact, nothing had ever felt as right and perfect as this moment, and she couldn't imagine anything ever would.

29

Racing back to the house, Greer quickly pulled off her maxi-dress and stepped into a short black Anna Sui. She didn't want to miss Brady's arrival at the after party, and she knew she didn't have a lot of time before the race ended. She struggled to reach the zipper in the back, straining her arm muscles in the process.

"Damn," she muttered as Jessica's mom appeared in the doorway. "Thank God," Greer exclaimed. "Can you help me with this?" She presented her back.

Aunt Claire came forward slowly and zipped her up. Greer turned to thank her and caught the expression on her face. She realized her aunt hadn't said a word since she arrived. Greer froze. "What's wrong? Is Jessi okay?"

Her aunt nodded and led her to Jessica's bed, where they sat facing each other. Dread spread up Greer's spine.

"Greer, honey, I have some bad news," her aunt began hesitantly. She picked up Greer's hand and held it firmly. "I spoke to your mother while you were out."

In that moment, Greer knew. This was it — the news she'd expected every minute of every day all summer.

"She and your dad . . . they're getting a divorce. She wants to speak to you herself, of course, but she wanted me to prepare you, in case you needed . . ." She didn't finish.

Greer stared at a point on the wall beyond her aunt's right shoulder. Each word hit her like a devastating blow. Her parents were splitting up. It was real.

"Why didn't she call me?" she asked dully.

Aunt Claire looked uncomfortable. "She had a function to attend, sweetie."

Greer knew that her mother had simply passed off the distasteful task to her softhearted sister-in-law. She looked down at her hand, still encased by her aunt's.

"Thanks, Aunt Claire," she said. "I think I'd like to be alone."

Her aunt nodded and hugged her tightly. Greer sat motionless as her aunt closed the door behind her. Flashbacks played in her mind of when she was younger. Vacations abroad, just the three of them, relaxed and happy.

Her father used to tickle her. He would dance with her mother whenever a Sinatra song came on. They always blew out birthday candles together, a tradition as old as she was. The family she knew — the life she knew — officially was no more.

Hot tears spilled down her perfectly bronzed cheeks as she stood, resolved. She needed to escape, to think about anything else. And Brady was waiting for her. Perfect, strong Brady. Fleeing down the stairs, she made for the darkening beach, where the after party was in full swing a short distance away. She swiped at her tears as she walked.

As she reached the fringes of the party, she saw people in sailing clothes among the crowd. The race must be over.

She headed for the staging tent. One of the groups of guys she passed had clearly placed in the regatta, judging by their matching polo shirts and level of mildly drunk happiness. One of them held out a full shot glass for her, but she ignored it. "I'm looking for Brady Stewart. Have you seen him?"

The guy nodded and pointed at an area away from the tent. "*Kaitlyn* won. He's in the victory circle with the Howards. The ceremony, pictures, all that stuff. It could take a while. Take a shot with us while you wait!"

Greer felt her tears threatening to rise again. She nodded and took the glass, draining it before the guy could pour one of his own. He looked surprised when she set the empty glass down next to his, but dutifully refilled it.

"Hey, guys, we've got a partyer here!" he shouted to his friends. They cheered and gathered around her, toasting. The whiskey shots came in quick succession. They went down warm and bitter. Two. Three. Four.

An hour later, Greer felt a little better as the liquor took the edge off. But as her clarity faded, her anger grew. Brady had said he would meet her at the party, and instead he was spending the whole night with his *ex*-girlfriend and her family. Greer needed to tell him about her parents, to get his reassurance that things would be okay. But he was with Kaitlyn. When Greer needed him most. She looked bleakly at the shot glass in her hand. At the end of the day, she was all alone, as usual.

She dropped the glass and staggered in the direction of the winner's circle, ignoring the protests from her new drinking buddies. She had trouble navigating through the crowd, but she kept her eyes on the bright floodlights ahead.

Suddenly, her toes caught on something, and she stumbled forward, falling roughly on her hands and knees. Strong arms seized her from behind and pulled her upright. She turned around slowly, recognizing the guy's laugh before she saw his face. Liam. He smiled down at her, keeping an arm tight around her waist.

"Are you okay?"

Greer scowled at him. "I don't need you to save me."

"I wasn't trying to save you. But a beautiful girl trips, I'm going to help her up."

"Whatever. I have to go." She pulled his arm off her waist.

"Hang on a second," he coaxed, taking hold of her arm. "What are you in such a hurry for?"

She looked at him intently. The crowd behind him blurred into patches of moving color. Where *was* she going? To storm into a victory celebration? Brady was with his perfect family and his perfect girl, celebrating his perfect win, the way it was obviously meant to be. Greer didn't fit into that equation, not with *her* family. And it's not like Brady had come looking for her to share the moment. He wanted something that she couldn't offer. Normalcy.

Liam rubbed her arm slowly. "God, you're sexy as hell, you know that? I thought that the first time I met you."

A crack of thunder boomed across the beach and two large droplets of water hit Greer in the face. Cries of dismay rose around them as people scrambled to gather their things. Greer swayed as Liam looked down at her, smiling charmingly. There was no confusion here. At least Liam's lust was obvious. She didn't have to guess how he felt about her. He was so simple.

Brady, her parents, everything else was so complicated. She just wanted to forget all of it, even just for a minute. As if reading her thoughts, Liam nudged her toward the darkness beyond the edge of the party. She allowed him to guide her into the woods, not caring enough to object. At least she didn't have to think.

When Greer stumbled out of the cover of the forest twenty minutes later, she blinked blearily in the heavy rain and bright lights. Her mind was spinning too dizzily for her to focus on the simmering disgust she felt with herself. She made her way toward the remnants of the party. Realizing her dress was still unzipped, she paused, reaching back in vain to close it. At the sound of a twig snapping in front of her, she spun around.

Jessi stood frozen, staring. She took in the mud-stained dress and legs. Her eyes quickly moved behind Greer, where Liam had chosen that moment to emerge from the trees, equally dirt-streaked. Greer's spinning head abruptly leveled itself. A flood of shame hit her like concrete, and she stared back at Jessica, at a loss for words.

"You — you slut!" Jessi cried, the accusation piercing the sound of the rain hitting the ground.

"No, you don't understand —"

"How could you?" Jessi sobbed, then whirled around and ran.

Greer felt indignant. Like she was the only slut in the Tuttle family. Impulsively, she shouted at Jessica's retreating back, "Oh, grow up, Jessi! Why don't you go find your precious Lara and ask her about what she's been doing with Drew?"

Ten yards away, Jessi ground to a halt and glanced back, then took off again, faster. Immediately feeling ugly and petty, Greer started after her. She hadn't taken two steps when she stopped, shocked.

Brady stood less than twenty feet away. He looked from her to Liam, revulsion twisting his face.

"Brady, let me explain," she began, walking toward him.

He held his hands up and backed away, shaking his head in disbelief. "You're unbelievable," he told her, disgust in his voice. "I thought we were actually getting somewhere. Have you been doing him this whole time?"

"No, it was a mistake," she cried. "It didn't happen the way you think."

"I think it happened exactly the way I think," he replied, the sarcasm dripping from his voice. "Was I up next? Because I'll pass on the honor of sloppy seconds."

She was stunned at the venom in his voice. He sounded like a different person. Her temper blazed.

"How dare you say that to me when you were with your psycho ex-girlfriend all night," she hissed. "You didn't even bother to look for me. Because you were with *her*!" The crescendo of her shouting caught the attention of a few people in the nearby tent, but she didn't care.

The fire went out in Brady's eyes. The anger was replaced with hurt. "I was with Kaitlyn and her family because we won the regatta," he explained. "I had to stay for the ceremony. And also to thank the Howards for letting me crew their boat, even after I broke up with their daughter. I was being polite to people I've known since I was five. I figured you were in the audience feeling happy for me."

Greer stood still, frozen into silence by the simple honesty of his explanation. With her defensiveness draining away, she couldn't think of anything to say. She knew there was a reason why she did what she did, but through the drinks and anger and sadness, she couldn't think of what it was.

"I don't think there's anything left to say," he said sadly, turning away.

She found her voice. "Wait," she called. "I think if we just talk about it —"

He shook his head. "There's nothing to talk about. I was right about you when we first met," he said, smiling ruefully. "I had hoped you'd prove me wrong." He shrugged, as if he'd learned his lesson.

Each word felt like a hammer . . . *Thud. Thud. Thud.*

Tears sprang to her eyes and collected in her throat,

making each breath heavy and ragged. She watched as he left her to return to the bright lights and happy people, helpless to stop him. The finality in his voice kept her rooted where she was. Standing in the drenching downpour, she didn't want to ever move again. Besides, there was nowhere for her to go.

Already in her pajamas, Lara sat Indian-style on her bed, scrolling through the pictures on her camera. She smiled when she came to the close-up of Drew that she'd taken that first day on the pier. At the memory of their first time together she felt a warm glow. So this was what it felt like to be in love.

She looked up as the door burst open, but her dreamy smile faded as soon as she saw Jessica's red-rimmed eyes and rain-soaked dress. "What happened?" she asked, concerned.

Jessica's voice shook. "You won't believe me. But first I have to ask you something crazy."

Lara nodded.

Jessica avoided her eyes. "It's stupid but . . . you . . . and Drew. My brother . . . You're not —?"

Oh, no. Lara couldn't stop the panic in her eyes. Recognition crossed over Jessica's face, and Lara knew it was too late to try to deny it. She never wanted it to come out like this. How had she even found out?

"I'm sorry. I wanted —" Lara began.

"When did it start? How long has everyone known about it but me?" Jessica interrupted shrilly, the pain in her eyes turning to anger.

"The day we met," Lara said quietly, fidgeting with a string on her patchwork duvet. "Before we found out we were stepcousins."

Greer appeared in the doorway, drenched, her black dress ruined. For an instant, the three of them were frozen in a tableau of guilt and anger.

"How long has Greer known?" she demanded, pointing accusingly at the sad, mud-stained figure near the door.

Lara took a deep breath. *Oh. Great.* "I told her last week. I wasn't trying to keep it from you —"

"But you did!" Jessica cried. She looked like she'd been punched in the stomach. "You were lying to my face all this time! How could you hook up with my *brother*?"

"You don't understand!" Lara's voice rose with frustration. Jessica didn't know what she'd gone through the past six weeks. "It was too complicated to just —"

Jessica scoffed. "I don't believe you!" she shouted. "Telling the truth isn't all that complicated. How could you think that *lying* would make me feel *better*?"

"I'm sorry, I never meant to hurt you," Lara insisted. All of the warmth and happiness she'd felt just a couple minutes ago felt like a distant memory.

"Right," Jessica mocked. "Lying, sneaking around with your *cousin* —"

Lara's patience snapped. "He's not my cousin," she said harshly. "I didn't even know him *or* you until a few weeks ago, so stop fantasizing that we're actually related!"

Jessica stepped back, her eyes wide with hurt.

"Jessica, I'm sorry," Greer cut in, stepping forward and shutting the door. She looked at Jessica squarely. "I was drunk and my par —"

"I don't want to hear it," Jessica sobbed, her voice shaking with rage. "I feel like I don't even know either of you! Why did you even pretend to care?"

The sorrow in her voice curbed Lara's anger. She stood and reached out for Jessica, who pulled away. "We weren't pretending," she insisted quietly.

Jessica shook her head violently. "I don't ever want to talk to either of you again."

Greer stepped in front of the door to prevent Jessica from storming out. "Liam never wanted you, Jessi. Everyone but you could see that!"

Lara's jaw dropped. She looked at Greer's mud-covered dress and understood. She put a hand on Jessica's arm to calm her down. Jessica didn't react. She just stood stonily.

"Look at yourself before you judge everyone else, *Jessi*," Greer sneered. "You threw yourself at Liam over and over. Don't blame me if he didn't want a desperate little girl just looking for attention."

Jessica wrenched her arm from Lara's grasp and slapped Greer's face. The crack reverberated through the room, stunning them all for a moment. Greer cried out and lunged, her hands clawing in front of her.

Just then, the door flew open and Jessica's mother rushed into the room, seizing Greer from behind. Lara grabbed Jessica, holding her arms back with all her strength.

"What is going on?" Jessica's mother demanded, looking back and forth between them. "Jessica, Greer, stop it *right now!*"

Breathing hard, the girls stopped struggling but continued to glare viciously at each other. Jessica's mother stepped between them to break their eye contact. Jessica pushed away from Lara's arms and stood defiantly.

"That's it," Jessica's mother said with finality. "This summer was a mistake. We are not doing this again. No way."

"What do you mean?" Jessica asked her mother. She was suddenly frantic. "We've always come here, this is part of our family."

Her mother looked at her coldly. "And your behavior tonight — is that what family means to you?" she asked. She didn't wait for an answer. "The decision is made, Jessica. This is the last summer at Pebble Beach."

Jessica slumped onto her bed in defeat. All of her anger had drained away, and Lara resisted the urge to go over to her.

"Get your pajamas," her mother told her. "You'll stay on the pull-out in our room. We've had enough drama for one night."

Silently, Jessica gathered her things.

"I don't want to hear another sound from this room," her mother warned. "Lara and Greer, I'll speak to your mothers in the morning."

Greer snorted. "I'll be gone by morning."

"No, you will not." Aunt Claire scanned the table and spied Greer's car keys with the rhinestone-encrusted Mercedes-Benz symbol. Greer groaned as Aunt Claire slid them into the pocket of her robe. "Your mother entrusted us with your care, and you will stay here and behave." She turned to include Lara in her steely glare. "I'll let your mother deal with you."

She paused in the doorway as she steered Jessica out. "You girls are family. You should value that. It's a shame you weren't able to learn that this summer."

No one replied. Jessica's mother shut the door with a solid bang. The finality echoed through the room. It was a sound Lara knew all too well. The sound of an ending.

31

Jessica's new favorite activity was to lie apathetically on the porch swing, with one leg hooked over the back. The rain had fallen steadily for days now with no sign of letting up, and she found herself idly fascinated by the downpour. Opened on her lap was one of the books on her summer reading list, *The House of Mirth,* but she wasn't reading. It was just a cover for what she really wanted to do: nothing.

As she swung back and forth, she thought bitterly that her current state was the exact opposite of how she'd started the summer. It was also the worst ending possible to her Pebble Beach memories. She'd tried to change their minds, but her parents had informed the landlord that they weren't going to renew their lease. Her dream for the summer had become a nightmare, thanks to Greer and Lara. They had no concept of how much she loved it here, what this place meant to her. Neither of them had even wanted to come to Pebble Beach, and now they'd fixed it so that none of them ever would again.

Jessica traced an errant raindrop that had landed on her outstretched leg. She hadn't spoken to Lara or Greer in five days. They'd staked out their respective territories — Jessica's was the porch — and kept out of one another's way. She assumed that Lara was with Drew somewhere, since she hadn't seen much of him, either. And as for Greer — she didn't care.

She opened the book to a random page. She'd read enough to know that Lily Bart was poor but pretended to be rich to meet a husband. The idea of a girl trying hard to get a guy felt uncomfortably familiar. She tossed the book on the table as a car turned into the driveway. The thumping bass of a Rhianna song forced its way through the closed windows, and the car came to a stop. Jessica felt a prickle of curiosity.

The car door swung open and a beautiful girl with long blonde hair eased out. Jessica did a double take. Ella!

With a shriek, Jessica bolted from the porch and ran over to her cousin. Ella ran, too, and they met in the middle, hugging fiercely for a long moment.

"Ella, you have no idea how glad I am to see you," Jessica said feverishly. Ella was a junior at Northeastern University in Boston. Jessica hadn't seen her since Ella had visited a friend at Cornell last year.

As they walked toward the porch, their arms around each other's waists, Ella drew back, concern shadowing her pretty face. "What's wrong, sweetie? You look upset."

Jessica rolled her eyes, feeling the threat of tears. "I don't even know where to start."

Ella grabbed her hand and smiled reassuringly. "I'm starving, anyway. You can tell me everything on the way to Red's. I've had dreams about those lobster rolls."

They raced back through the rain and dove into Ella's car. Ella jammed the car into reverse and cut the deafening music. When they were on the highway, she glanced at Jessica. "Okay, start from the beginning."

That would be the day my parents said we were coming back here, Jessica realized. She explained how she'd watched Ella and the other older cousins have the best summers every year on Pebble Beach, and how much she had wanted that for herself. She told Ella about Lara and Greer. And, of course, everything about Liam, her summer boy that wasn't. Ella let Jessica talk on and on, only occasionally prompting her with "mm-hmms" and "ahs" when appropriate. She was the perfect listener.

Jessica hadn't even gotten to regatta day when they arrived at Red's. "Hold that thought," Ella commanded. She ran out, huddling under the dripping awning. Jessica glanced around. The tables were predictably empty, but a surprising number of cars contained people hunched over their sandwiches. She couldn't really blame them.

Ella returned with a bulging paper bag. She handed Jessica an overstuffed roll and unwrapped one for herself. "Oh, God," she sighed as she chewed. "I can't believe how good these still are. Okay, keep going."

Between bites, Jessica spilled every last, gory detail, all the way through the fight.

"And the next day, my parents told Mr. Selden that we wouldn't be back," she finished miserably.

Ella was silent for a moment. "That's a lot for one summer," she said at last. "Oh, Jess — I'm sorry you got hurt. But it'll get better, believe me."

Tears welled up in Jessica's eyes again. "I wanted one of the perfect summers you guys always had — the boys, the parties, the cousins hanging out together. Now I'll never have that chance again."

Ella stared at her in disbelief. "What makes you think our summers were perfect, Jess?" She shook her head. "You were too young. You didn't see everything."

Through her tears, Jessica looked at her cousin curiously. "What do you mean?"

Leaning her head back against the headrest, Ella looked solemnly at the ceiling of the car. "You have no idea how much drama we went through back then. Broken hearts, lying, boyfriend stealing, you name it. We completely hated each other a lot of the time."

Dumbfounded, Jessica digested this new information. "It couldn't have been that bad."

Ella laughed. "Are you kidding? My big lesson from living with the Tuttle cousins? Try looking from someone else's point of view. And remember that everyone makes mistakes. Even you, I'd imagine."

Jessica squirmed uncomfortably in her seat as she remembered Connor.

Ella patted her on the shoulder. "Look, you have every right to be angry. But speaking from experience, the anger fades, and the boys come and go. Your family is one of the only things that you can really count on."

"Well, I definitely can't count on boys," Jessica muttered, staring at the windshield. The cool rain outside had caused the glass to fog up.

Ella squeezed her hand. "Sweetie, I'm really sorry you got your heart broken," Ella said solemnly. "But I have to say that's pretty standard for Pebble Beach. We all ended up licking our wounds come September." She sighed. "Even in college."

Jessica didn't know if she could live through another

summer like this one. "So what was the point?" she wondered aloud. All her planning, the makeover, the Liam detective work — it had all ended in disaster.

Ella smiled. "I think the point is that you made two amazing friends who also happen to be your cousins. You're the Summer Girls of Pebble Beach, 2.0!"

Jessica laughed at her enthusiasm, remembering that she'd used that exact same phrase. "I guess. Hey, Ella? Thanks for listening."

Ella leaned over and hugged her tightly. "Anytime." She sat back in her seat. "Ready to go back?"

Jessica nodded and Ella started the car, wiping the mist off the windshield. The raindrops blurred the view, but they could still make out Red's squat little shack in front of them. Ella eyed her cousin, her hand on the ignition. "But wait. How about a second round? Who knows when we'll be back here again, right?"

Jessica grinned broadly for the first time that day. "Right."

Laughing, they opened the car doors and ran out shrieking into the cleansing summer rain.

32

Lara's stomach growled insistently. After five days, her digestive system still hadn't gotten used to its new schedule. Since the fight, she'd holed up in her room and deliberately avoided going downstairs during mealtimes. Fortunately, Greer only came in to sleep and change, which she did quickly and silently.

Lara checked her watch. It was just after three o'clock. The coast should be clear. She tiptoed downstairs and into the kitchen, which was mercifully empty. She rooted around in the fridge and emerged with a peach yogurt, a slice of cold pizza, and some leftover curry chicken salad. Perfect. She gathered up her findings, along with a fork and spoon, and took them outside to the deck. It was raining, but she wanted to be alone and, fortunately, there was only room for one under the umbrella.

Nibbling on the pizza, she looked down on the deserted beach. The rain had darkened the sand and agitated the water, making the landscape look cold and forbidding. There were only a couple of weeks left of summer, and it seemed it might rain all the way through to the finish. The sound of the sliding glass door opening caused her to pause in her chewing, but she didn't turn around.

"Lara?" It was Drew.

She looked up and swallowed her pizza. He stood in the rain, looking sad and serious. Her heart ached at the sight of him, and she glanced down to control her emotions. He hadn't come to see her since their night together, but she knew he'd heard about her fight with Jessica. She could tell by his expression that her tiny flame of hope was about to be extinguished.

"Hi," she finally responded.

"Can I sit?"

"Yeah, sure." She shifted over so that there was room on the dry part of the bench.

He sat. "Thanks." Resting his hands on the table, he looked at them for a moment. She could tell he was trying to figure out the right words.

"Let me save you the trouble," she preempted. "I know what you're going to say."

He looked at her then, the pain in his eyes sadly familiar. "I'm sorry, Lara. It's just too hard."

She nodded, feeling oddly numb. "I understand." She wondered if it would be rude if she got up and left.

"We just had the shittiest luck in the world."

She nodded again. She could go on nodding forever. But she really wished he would just stop talking.

"I quit Ahoy this morning," he continued. Startled, Lara stopped nodding and looked at him. "I'm going to work at Jordan's camp for the rest of the summer."

Well, there it was. Drew Tuttle had neatly swept himself out of her life. He would no longer live or work here. Next summer, she'd either have no family or a brand-new family. She would probably never see him again. The finality was devastating.

Drew stood up when she maintained her silence. "I've got to go pack." He paused. "Bye, Lara."

She nodded one more time.

And then he left.

Should I run after him? Grab his pant leg and beg him not to go? She felt like she was supposed to do something dramatic that involved wailing, but instead she continued to eat her lunch. First the pizza, then the yogurt, and finally the curry chicken, with the raisins picked out. When she was finished, she took her trash into the kitchen. Then she found her mother in the house next door, reading in a chair by her bedroom window.

Her mother put down her book as Lara entered. "Hi, honey."

Lara sat on the bed, facing her. "Mom, I know what's been going on. I just need to tell you that I can't keep doing this."

Her mom looked puzzled. "Keep doing what?"

Lara swept her hand around, indicating the room, the house, all of it. "This. I can't keep going along for the ride every time you decide to give up on one husband and find another."

Her mother's eyes widened. "Lara, where is this coming from?"

"I'm not stupid, Mom. I can smell when another divorce looms."

"Lara, sweetie. We're not getting divorced."

Lara looked up, surprised at her mother's unusually firm tone. "But I heard you and Mike fighting."

"You heard *a* fight," her mother continued. "Husbands and wives fight, Lara. So do mothers and daughters, and cousins apparently. Just because families fight doesn't mean that we're finished with each other. As long as they want to work things out, they do."

Lara thought she'd misheard. "You're not getting

divorced," she echoed. She didn't know whether to laugh or cry.

Her mother's voice turned gentle. "Look, I know this fight you had with Jessica and Greer rattled you, but you girls need to work it out."

"I don't know if that's possible," Lara admitted, moving over so her mom could take a seat next to her.

"From what I've seen of this family, a little time heals all wounds. Apologies come in pretty handy as well." Her mom smiled and squeezed her shoulder. "Think of all the fun you were having before the fight. I don't know if I'd ever seen you so happy."

Lara considered, swinging her leg against the cherry-wood night table. She *had* been happy in this family. Then her heart sank. She remembered what she'd said to Jessica that night. That they weren't even related. Lara cringed. The truth was, other than her mom, the Tuttles were the only family that she'd ever really wanted to belong to.

Her mother was quiet, allowing Lara to think. "I guess I should find Jessica," Lara said at last.

Lara's mom nodded in agreement. "I think that's an excellent idea," she pronounced. "But it can wait a little longer, don't you think?"

She was confused. "Why?"

Her mother smiled mischievously, looking ten years younger than her age. They could look like sisters, with the same bright blue eyes. "Mike owes me a date night. Why don't the three of us go out, just our little family?" She beamed, obviously proud of her plan.

Lara curled up next to her mother and laid her head on her chest. She could hear the slow, steady heartbeat that must have soothed her when she was a baby. "That's a great idea," she murmured contentedly. "Anywhere but Ahoy. I hear the service stinks."

"I'm sorry, dear, but I can't have you alone in the apartment. What kind of mother would I be?" Cassandra Hallsey's laugh tinkled down the line. "I'll be back from St. Barth's before you know it."

Greer jammed the cell phone between her ear and shoulder so she could rip open a sugar packet for her third coffee of the day. She was sitting in the Lookout Diner, her refuge for the moment. She'd spent the past few days all over Pebble Beach — the bookstore, the Okay Café, but avoiding Ahoy. Aunt Claire still had her car keys, so her options were limited.

Greer bit her lip in frustration. "Why can't I just stay home with Maria?" she asked. It's not like she hadn't been dumped on the housekeeper before.

"Maria's on vacation this week," her mother reminded her.

An idea struck Greer as she set down her little silver coffee spoon. "Why don't I go down to St. Barth's with you?" she asked excitedly. "We could spend some time together since I've been away all summer." It was a very un-Greer-like sentiment, but since she learned of the divorce, she'd felt an inexplicable need to call her mother every day.

"I don't think that's a good idea, Greer. I need some quiet time to decompress."

The buzz of conversation and clinking plates suddenly seemed very loud. It was obvious her mother had her own plans, and they didn't include her daughter. Greer felt helpless, trapped in this New England hellhole.

"Have you spoken to your father?" Her mother's tone was carefully neutral.

"No," Greer snapped. She hated it when her parents pumped her for information about each other. The truth was, she'd spoken to her father fifteen minutes ago. He was about to go windsurfing and had to run. She didn't bother asking if she could stay with him and his "friend." There was no doubt that three was a crowd in *that* case.

"I'll tell you what always makes me feel better, darling. Take your father's credit card and do some shopping. Buy yourself a fun new bag." There was a rustling sound. "When I get back from the islands, we'll have some mother-daughter time together at Georgette Klinger. How does that sound?"

Greer didn't bother to answer. She could tell her mother had already checked out of the conversation.

"All right, I've got to go find my passport. I could have sworn it was in my Birkin. I'll call you when I get back. Kisses."

"Bye." Greer ended the call and stared at her phone. She wondered if there was anyone else to call. She'd already asked four of her most reliable boys to come and rescue her from utter boredom, but they were working or on vacation. One offered to drive up for the weekend, but she'd hoped to be gone by then, so she put him on standby.

She turned her phone around in her hands. The mirror on the back showed her reflection, one that last week's Greer would have been appalled to see. Her hair was lank and greasy, and she wore no makeup. Dark circles shadowed her eyes. *I look like I feel,* she thought. She eyed the group of boys in the booth diagonally across from hers, but they gave no indication of noticing her. For the first time that she could remember, she was invisible to guys. It probably didn't help that she was wearing shapeless yoga pants and a huge, tentlike rain jacket that she'd swiped from the hook by the front door. Surprisingly, she didn't mind. It actually felt comforting to blend into the background, for once.

She considered her mother's advice, but with the rain and lack of transportation, she ruled out a shopping spree. Besides, Greer hadn't called her parents for that. She'd hoped that her father's departure would inspire some mother-daughter bonding, or that her father would suddenly remember that he had a daughter. *No on both counts.*

She she couldn't help remembering the last time she saw Brady's parents. They were so . . . *parental.* She was sure that, even in the unlikely event of their divorce, their first priorities would be Clara and Brady. That was the way it was supposed to be. Greer sighed. She'd tried not to think about Brady in the past few days. Every time he seeped into her thoughts, she'd pushed him away. But wasn't that what her parents were doing? Trying to ignore the painful and distasteful? Greer knew how that attitude hurt those around them, aka *her.*

She stared out the window, the trails of raindrops obscuring the view of the street. Finally allowing herself to think about Brady, she felt the full spectrum of her anger, guilt, regret, and sorrow. Brady was still under the assumption that she was a coldhearted, indiscriminating slut. The knowledge made her heart hurt. She'd tried so hard to get him to see that she wasn't who he initially thought. And he'd repaid her by actually liking her for the person she was, not just the way she looked. *He must think it was all a game to me* — which was so far from the truth that it was absurd, even if she was the only one who knew it.

Suddenly, Greer knew what she had to do. She put money down on the dingy yellow table and left the diner, quickly passing the boys who were flirting with the table of girls nearby. She turned in the direction of Brady's house, which was next to the yacht club.

The house was straight out of *Country Living*, picket fence included. Now that she was here, she felt intimidated. Hesitantly, she rang the doorbell and waited.

Brady opened the door, looking heartbreakingly adorable in a white Polo shirt. His blond hair was tousled, and he looked very surprised to see her.

Greer screwed up her courage.

"Can I talk to you?"

He shook his head as his surprise faded to annoyance. "I don't think that's a good idea. Sorry."

Before he could slam the door on her, she put up her hand. "I know I don't deserve it after what I did, but I'm asking you to give me the chance to apologize. That's all."

He stood still for a moment. She held her breath. She was counting on Brady's innately good heart.

Finally, silently, he stepped aside to let her in. Grateful, she entered and stood dripping in the entryway. He led her to the kitchen and brought her a thick towel. She knew she looked like a drowned rat, but it didn't matter. He sat opposite her at the table and looked at her, waiting.

She'd rehearsed the things she wanted to say, but now that the moment had come, she couldn't find the words. Feeling a little desperate, she started anyway. "Brady, I'm so sorry." She looked in his eyes as she spoke. "What I did was unforgivable. I'm messed up, I know that. I think it runs in my family. I honestly didn't mean to hurt you."

He raised his eyebrows. "'Runs in your family'?"

She took a deep breath. "I lied to you about my parents. My father's having an affair with a college student, and my mother's oblivious to anything but spending his money. They don't care about anyone but themselves. We're all walking disasters." She laughed humorlessly. "We're about as dysfunctional as you can get."

Brady looked confused. "Why would you lie about something like that? I don't get it."

Greer smiled ruefully. "I guess I didn't want to be the person you were so convinced I was. The crazy, screwed-up city girl."

He looked at her skeptically. "Then why did you — Liam?" He spat out the name.

"I had just found out that my parents are getting divorced." Brady looked up, startled, but didn't interrupt. "I was really angry and I got drunk. I was looking for you, and then I found out you were with Kaitlyn. And Liam was there and . . ." She shrugged. "It's not an excuse, it's not. But you have to know that I didn't plan to hurt you."

Brady was quiet for a moment, considering. "You don't have to be like them," he offered. "I admit that I thought you were the typical rich bitch who walks all over guys, but you turned out to be smart and funny and caring." He smiled and continued, more quietly. "I'm glad I know what happened that night. I felt like I'd been a fool all summer."

Greer shook her head, sending droplets of rain flying across the table. "Brady, you weren't a fool. What I felt for you was real. Maybe I just didn't know how to handle it. It was new to me, too."

Brady cocked his head. "There's one thing I don't get. Why did you think that knowing about your parents would make me like you less? That doesn't make any sense."

"Because your family is so perfect," Greer explained reluctantly. "I didn't think I would fit into your perfect life."

"Perfect life? What are you talking about?"

"This!" She gestured around the enormous country kitchen with framed portraits of Clara and Brady on the walls. "Your house, your family, your yacht club, your sailing, even your ex-girlfriend. I'm shocked you don't have a golden retriever named Rover."

Brady smiled and leaned back in his chair. "We have a cat named Truffles, if that helps."

Greer groaned. "You know what I mean. How could I tell you about my mother's Botox obsession when your mother probably bakes cookies in her sleep?" She pulled the towel closer around her, feeling awkwardly exposed, even though she was fully dressed.

Brady laughed, shaking his head. "You have no clue what you're talking about."

She glared at him. "Don't laugh at me."

"There's no such thing as perfect, Greer." Brady looked a little embarrassed. "My parents have had separate bedrooms since I was ten years old." He looked at the ceiling, covering his eyes for a moment. "God, I can't believe I'm telling you this."

"That's a little weird," Greer admitted. In some sick way, hearing that made her feel a bit better.

He focused on her. "And your family's pretty cool. Jessica, Lara — they're awesome."

"Oh." She nodded soberly. "Right. Well, I'm not so sure they consider me family at this point."

Brady reached across the table and took her hand. "Don't worry. The thing with family is that they're stuck with you, no matter what crap you pull."

Greer looked at him in awe. After everything she'd done to him, how had this turned into him trying to make her feel better? "Brady," she said, her voice catching. "Can we get past this?" She felt the hope flaring in her eyes.

"Greer," he said, sitting back in his chair. "Listen to me. You're amazing. And up until this last week, this summer has been . . . unexpected." He paused. "But I really do need to be alone for a while."

She met his eyes and nodded, too disappointed to speak. She hadn't expected to just go back to the way things were, but it still hurt — a lot. They both stood and she picked up her bag. Suddenly, he stepped closer. He pressed his lips gently on hers for a long moment. Greer closed her eyes, losing herself in his warm, familiar arms until they broke apart. She left him sitting in the kitchen as she started the long journey back to the house.

34

Lara put the finishing touches on her creation and stood back to study it critically. She nodded, then picked up the tray. She headed straight to the front porch, walking quickly in case she lost her nerve. She had a little trouble balancing the tray in one hand while opening the door with the other, but managed somehow.

"Voilà," she cried, stepping out onto the porch. Jessica was sitting on the swing with a gorgeous blonde girl who actually resembled Jessica a great deal. It must have been Ella. Lara's mother had mentioned that she had shown up. Seeing her and Jessica looking so close produced a stab of jealousy. Not too long ago, Lara would have been on that swing with Jessica.

As if reading her thoughts, Ella stood up and winked. "You must be Lara, right? I'll go make sure the adults are behaving," she said, quickly disappearing through the glass door.

Jessica looked at Lara curiously. *At least that's better than all-consuming hatred*, Lara thought. She placed the tray on the low table in front of the swing and sat down. "It's a peace offering," she explained.

Jessica studied the massive bowl overflowing with three flavors of ice cream, bananas, hot fudge, nuts, whipped cream, and five cherries. "What is it?"

"It's a banana split!" Lara feigned shock.

Still examining the creation like it was about to come to life at any moment, Jessica cocked her head quizzically. "But why?"

Lara grinned. "Remember when you nearly let me drown just to prove a point?"

A smile flitted across Jessica's face. "I remember."

"Well, after my failure you bought me a banana split. That was the moment I first felt like part of your family." She paused thoughtfully. "Part of *any* family, really. So I'm returning the favor."

Jessica nodded, looking more open.

Lara plunged ahead. "I'm so sorry for not being honest with you. I should've told you about Drew. I don't know what I was thinking."

Jessica shook her head. "No, you were right. I'm sorry for freaking out like I did. It's just gross to think about you and Drew."

"Of course," Lara said. "Drew and I didn't know we were cousins until after we already liked each other. After that, we talked ourselves into thinking that it wasn't a big deal." She looked away. "It's over now, in case you were wondering."

Jessica was quiet as she picked up one of the spoons and handed it to Lara. "No sense letting this monstrosity go to waste," she said, changing the subject.

Lara grinned and they both dug in heartily. As Jessica popped a piece of caramel-drenched banana into her mouth, she sighed with pleasure. "This is so good. Where did you learn to make banana splits like this?"

"You've never heard of the 'Oh Boy Ahoy'?" Lara demanded, clutching at her chest. "It's one of the signature desserts at the fine establishment that so generously employs me. You should feel lucky that I didn't drop a scoop on the floor and then brush off the dirt. It would not have been the first time."

"Ew," Jessica squealed. "That has to be the grossest thing I ever heard."

"Grosser than me checking out your brother's butt at work every day?"

Jessica made unusually realistic retching noises while Lara continued eating blithely. When she recovered, she glared at her cousin. "Promise me that you'll never, *ever* refer to my brother's butt again."

"What if there's a bee about to sting him?" Lara asked playfully. "Or he's about to sit in a pool of melted chocolate? Am I supposed to just let it happen?"

"Yes," Jessica said firmly.

"Does that include Jordan, too?" she teased.

"Yes!" Jessica shouted in feigned anger. "Stop talking about my brothers!"

"Fine, fine." Lara waited a moment until Jessica relaxed. "Can we talk about Aunt Beatrice's butt? Because that's a *whole* lot of ground to cover."

They collapsed into hysterical giggles, making the porch swing sway precariously. When the fit had passed, they slouched lazily, breathing hard.

Jessica stood and extended a hand to Lara. "Come on. It's time you officially met our cousin Ella. She can tell us about all the drama that went on when she was here. It almost makes our summer look pretty boring."

Lara raised an eyebrow. "This I've gotta hear."

She grasped the offered hand and hauled herself up, nearly pulling Jessica down in the process. Laughing, they entered the house together, arm in arm.

Greer had just gotten out of the shower and was standing in a towel when her bedroom door opened and Lara came in. As soon as she saw her cousin's face, a million things came to her mind. There was so much she wanted to say.

"Lara, I —" she began.

"Hey, let's —" Lara started at exactly the same time.

They stopped and looked at each other, then burst into surprised laughter. Lara hurdled a pile of Greer's shoes in the middle of the floor and wrapped Greer in a hug. Greer stood as stiffly as she always did.

"I'm sorry for telling Jessi," Greer told her when they broke apart. "It was a bitchy thing to do."

Lara fell backward onto her bed. "Apology accepted, blah blah. Now let's move on. I'm bored out of my mind."

"That wasn't so bad. Now comes the hard part," Greer mused. "Jessi."

Lara nodded sympathetically. "We finally talked today."

Greer exhaled. "I should go look for her."

"She went to town with Ella," Lara supplied helpfully. "Good luck."

Greer ran through the downpour into the Okay Café. Inside, she spotted two flaxen-haired heads near the counter. She hadn't seen Ella in years, but her older cousin was as beautiful as ever. She and Jessica were laughing and poring over a menu, but Ella looked up at Greer as she approached their table.

"Hi," Greer said awkwardly. She hadn't counted on saying all of this in front of someone else, much less Ella.

Ella jumped up and hugged Greer, who was resigned to it now. When she was released, she turned to Jessica, hoping for an indication that she had suddenly contracted amnesia and forgotten the last week. No such luck. Jessica might not have been shooting daggers with her eyes, but she wasn't smiling either.

"Um, Jessi, I'd like to talk to you, if you don't mind." Greer was even more nervous than she had been when Brady opened his front door. The stakes were higher here. Jessi had to forgive her. They were family.

Ella looked between them. "I think I should give you two some privacy," she suggested. "I'll be at the counter. I'm not here to take sides." She flashed them an encouraging smile before walking away. They watched the young waiter's eyes bulge as he took her in. He nearly tripped over his feet to make her a free milk shake. Greer was impressed. Then she turned back to Jessica.

"Jessi, I said horrible things to you and what I did to you was even worse. I'm really, truly sorry. I hope you'll be able to forgive me one day," she said, a touch more formally than she'd intended.

Jessica studied her, searching her eyes. "You really hurt me," she said softly.

Greer brushed away her tears. "I didn't mean to. I know it doesn't make a difference, but it wasn't about Liam, or you. It could have been anyone. I was drunk and angry about my parents and he just happened to be there. I wasn't thinking."

"That's the thing. You *were* thinking — just not about anyone but yourself," Jessica pointed out coolly.

Greer flinched. She'd said the exact same thing about her parents all too recently. "You're right. I'm not looking for sympathy," she added quickly. "I just want you to know the mind-set I was in when I made that mistake. And it was a mistake. I knew it the minute I let it happen. I just wasn't strong enough to care at the time. All my caring was used up."

Her cousin's green eyes softened. "I heard about your parents. Are you okay?"

"Not really," Greer admitted, but changed the subject. She didn't want to lose her train of thought. "Also, I'm sorry for telling you about Lara and Drew the way that I did. It was a low blow."

Jessica grimaced. Apparently she wasn't quite over her revulsion.

Greer couldn't help smiling at her expression. It was so Jessi.

"Lara and I made up today." Jessica looked earnestly at her cousin. "I do want us to be friends again, Greer."

Greer felt a lump in her throat. "Me, too. Actually, I want to be *cousins* again."

Jessica nodded. Greer was relieved to see the usual happiness returning to her cousin's face. She didn't realize how much she'd missed it. "It's funny," Greer observed. "It took my parents splitting up to show me I actually do need my family."

"It's a good thing we're stuck with each other then," Jessica joked. She finally seemed to be back to her old self. Maybe even back to her old advice-needing self . . .

"You know," Greer began carefully, "while you were trying to get Liam's attention all summer, someone else was trying to get yours."

Jessica looked surprised. "Who?"

"Are you blind?" Greer had to laugh at her cousin's innocence. "Connor's totally in love with you."

"But we're just friends." The shock on Jessica's face was genuine.

"Not to him," Greer declared.

"Huh." Dumbfounded, Jessica sat back in the booth, lost in thought.

Ella descended on the table carrying a huge plate. "You two look a hundred times better than you did before." She set down the biggest napoleon slice Greer had ever seen. It practically qualified as a whole cake. Ella brandished three forks ceremoniously. "I want you both to know that the eating of a napoleon in the Okay Café has a long-standing tradition among Tuttle girls. It's a proven crisis food. The rule is, one napoleon, multiple forks." Greer shifted over so Ella could squeeze into the booth.

"Between Lara's banana split and this, I'm not going to fit into my fall clothes," Jessica groaned.

"Oh, come on," Greer laughed. "Live a little."

Ella scooped up a piece of the napoleon. She raised her fork. "To the Tuttle girls! We'll always be family, even if we hate one another's guts!" Greer and Jessica exchanged a smile as they held up their forks and stuck the napoleon in their mouths in perfect unison.

36

"This sun feels incredible," Jessica sighed, rolling onto her stomach lazily.

"Mmm," Greer agreed from beneath her enormous straw hat. "I think I'm melting."

"Did someone throw water on you?" Lara asked innocently, feeling her lips twitch.

Without raising her head, Greer Frisbee'd her phonebook-thick September *Vogue* in Lara's general direction, sending grains of sand flying over all three of them.

"Ow," Lara whined, rubbing her leg. "Must you be so brutal?"

"Ask Jessi," Greer suggested contentedly. "She's the one with the history of violence."

"I told you a million times I was sorry for slapping you,"

Jessica replied sourly from her spot between them. "Anyway, you should thank me. It saved you from having to put bronzer on that cheek for days."

Greer snorted as Lara sat up on her towel, impressed. "Look at you!" Lara exclaimed. "Glad to see my lessons in obnoxiousness are sinking in."

"Dear God, let's hope not," Greer remarked. "The last thing we need is a Lara clone yapping away and disturbing the peace."

Lara tossed the sunblock on Greer's exposed stomach, relishing the fun banter. "Not a clone. I was thinking more of a disciple."

After six solid days of drenching rain, the clouds had finally parted to reveal the relentless August sun. With a week and a half remaining in Pebble Beach, the girls had decided to hit the sand every day. After all their wounds had healed, they were even closer than before, and Lara couldn't have been more relieved. She'd even managed not to dwell too much on how much she missed Drew, who'd been with Jordan for the past week and hadn't been in touch.

"Guys, I have an idea," Jessica announced.

"What?" Greer asked, shading her eyes with her hands.

"Everyone's been so crabby that no one's planned an end-of-summer party," she said breathlessly. "This is our last chance."

"Last chance for what?" Lara asked, puzzled.

"To have the perfect summer." Jessica smiled serenely as her cousins groaned.

Greer propped herself up on her elbows to stare at Jessica. "Are you still hung up on that?" she asked incredulously.

"I hate to break it to you, Jess, but I think that ship has sailed," Lara agreed, feeling a pang of sorrow.

Jessica waved away their negativity. "We have to make the best of the time we have left, since we won't be together next year. I want the rest of our summer to really count."

From her prone position, Lara exchanged a guilty glance with Greer. She felt partly responsible for robbing Jessica of her beloved Pebble Beach summers, but there was nothing they could do.

"A party could be fun," Lara said thoughtfully. "It can't be worse than the adults' sad attempts."

"We could decorate, have games, organize sports," Jessica counted off on her hand, then shrugged. "Like Lara said, the bar is set pretty low right now."

"All right, I'm in," Greer declared. "I need a new project."

By the time they trooped back into the house, the girls had a fun, ambitious agenda planned — but they needed to do some major fund-raising. Just as they'd hoped, a bunch of the uncles were hanging out in the shade of umbrellas by the grill, including Uncle Mike and Jessica's dad. Greer took the lead, confidently approaching them with her most dazzling smile. Ten minutes later, Greer had a thick wad of cash and a promise to get the whole family to show up.

The next week flew by quickly, with the girls busy shopping, decorating, and planning. They kept the details of the party under wraps, wanting the family to be surprised. Lara knew that, despite Uncle Carr's promise to get the whole family to show up, Drew wouldn't be making an appearance. No one had mentioned any plans for him to come back. But Lara kept her sadness private. She wanted to enjoy the last few days of summer as much as anyone.

On the afternoon of the party, Lara, Greer, and Jessica ran through their checklists.

"I'm nervous," Jessica admitted before the girls went outside, her green eyes wide with anxiety. "This will be everyone's last memory of Pebble Beach," she explained. "I want them to have a good time."

"After all the work we did, they'd better," Greer said ominously.

Visibly screwing up her courage, Jessica led the way out back. She climbed onto a lawn chair and faced the gathered aunts, uncles, and little cousins. "Thanks for coming, everyone. Welcome to the 'Tuttles Invade Pebble Beach' end-of-summer party!"

Lara and Greer clapped and cheered, with the crowd joining in enthusiastically. The prospect of a party evidently had everyone in a good mood.

Jessica beamed at the applause. "I know that it isn't always easy spending so much time together in *really* close proximity. But even though we sometimes want to kill each other, we're lucky to be part of something as amazing as this family." She paused and smiled down at Lara and Greer, who grinned back.

"I wish this wasn't the end of our summers together, but we all have great memories that we can always look back on. I hope this party will be one of them. Lara, Greer, and I wanted to make sure our very last summer in Pebble Beach goes out with a bang. Let's get the party started!"

An eager buzz rose up as their relatives spilled onto the beach, where the girls had a section roped off for the party. They'd organized activities for everyone, young and old. Uncle Carr immediately challenged Uncle Frank to one-on-one beach volleyball, while Aunt Trudy and her little girls serenaded the party from the portable karaoke machine. Thanks to Lara's Ahoy connection, a traditional Maine clambake had been cooking since morning. The amazing aroma of lobsters, clams, potatoes, and corn steamed out of the fire pit. Lara grinned as family members fanned out, feeling a deep sense of accomplishment.

"Who's up for football?" Mike shouted.

Jessica and Lara looked at each other, their eyebrows raised. They each grabbed one of Greer's elbows and dragged her along. Despite her claim of unathleticism, Greer turned out to be an exceptionally good tackler, which Lara discovered while facedown in the sand.

"I'm quitting the team," Lara sputtered, trying to brush off her tongue after her third hit.

"Don't be such a whiner," Greer told her, grinning in satisfaction. "It's just a game."

"Not to you," Lara grumbled. "It's a vendetta."

As dusk settled on the beach, Lara, starving, traded contact sports for the buffet line. She filled a heaping plate and plopped down exhausted on the sand near her mom.

"Having fun?" Lara asked between bites of corn on the cob.

"You girls did a great job," her mom remarked with genuine awe. "I haven't seen everyone so happy since — well, since I've known them."

Lara smiled and wiped the butter from her face with the back of her hand. She laid her head on her mom's shoulders, feeling a kind of calm she wasn't sure she'd ever felt before.

Lara abandoned her food to search for Greer and Jessica. She found — or rather, *heard* — them massacring "Toxic" at the karaoke machine.

She felt an arm around her shoulders and turned to find Aunt Claire looking fondly at all of them. "I just wanted to let you girls know how proud I am of you. This party was obviously a lot of work. Everybody's raving about you."

The cousins grinned at one another. *They'd pulled it off!*

"In fact, you did *such* a good job promoting this beach that Carr and I realized how much we've been through out here. How much Pebble Beach means to our family," she continued. "And we're not the only ones. I think it was your little tearjerker speech," she added, smiling knowingly at her daughter.

"What does that mean?" Jessica asked, confusion clouding her face.

"It means that your father just got off the phone with Rob Selden. He's bringing the contracts over right now to sign on for next summer."

Lara felt joy and relief flood through her.

Jessica leaped to her feet, hugging her mother in a frenzy of happiness and excitement. She turned and threw herself on Lara and Greer next, nearly bowling them over with her fierce embrace. Lara wrapped her arms tight around her.

"We're coming back!" Jessica crowed, then stopped. "Will you guys come back, too?"

"I hope so!" Lara's life hadn't stayed stable for a full year in a long time, but she was optimistic about this one.

Jessica turned to Greer. "What about you?"

Lara assumed Greer's plans for next summer involved some coast with an unpronounceable name and topless beaches.

Greer rolled her eyes. "Of course," she snapped. "What would this place be without the Pebble *Bitch*?"

The girls cracked up and collapsed on the sand, their eyes watering. Suddenly, they heard a crackle. A giant burst of green appeared over their heads, momentarily illuminating dozens of surprised, upturned faces. The girls looked at each other and grinned. As the colorful fireworks lit the night sky, one after another, everyone around them oohed and aahed in delight.

"I'll let my dad know how much we enjoyed his contribution to the party." Greer smirked wickedly.

Lara shook her head. "You'd better, before he gets the bill and has a heart attack."

There was a moment of contented silence as the three girls took in the fireworks exploding in the darkness. It reminded Lara of the Fourth of July, when they had all bonded at Red's. An uncharacteristic lump rose in her throat and she reached out to squeeze Jessica's hand.

"Hey, Lara?" Jessica said softly, and Lara turned her head to meet her cousin's wide gaze. "I — I've noticed how, um, down you've seemed lately. And — I, um —" Jessica glanced at Greer, who nodded encouragingly. Lara realized they'd been talking about her, but this idea didn't anger her.

"I know it's because of Drew," Jessica finished, glancing awkwardly down at the sand. "I know you must miss him."

Lara felt her heart contract, then expand. "I do," she finally admitted. She could have sworn she heard Greer mutter, "Knew it."

Jessica gave Lara a small smile. "Look, I've been thinking about the situation a lot. And I guess being stepcousins isn't the same thing as being actual cousins. Except for you and me, of course."

Lara smiled back, the lump in her throat growing. "So . . ."

Jessica tucked her knees under her chin, looking thoughtful. "So I'll talk to Drew when we're both back at home. I have a feeling he's waiting for me to tell him I'm getting over the, you know, the grossness. And maybe I am. Or will."

"I understand," Lara said truthfully. She wasn't sure what the future held for her and Drew, but the knowledge that she'd probably be seeing him again next summer filled her with a surge of hope. "Hey, Greer?" she asked, wanting to take the focus off herself. "Have you heard from Brady?" Greer had filled her and Jessica in on her visit to Brady's house.

Greer nodded, biting her glossy bottom lip. "He actually texted me this morning, but I didn't want to say anything because we were all so crazed with the party. I think he and

243

I are going to be talking during the fall. We both need time, I guess. And Putney isn't too far from New York . . ." She trailed off, smiling.

Both Greer and Lara glanced at Jessica, who was hugging her knees and staring at the fireworks that boomed overhead. Then she blushed, looking over at her cousins.

"Well, I think I'm off boys for the moment," she said, and although Lara knew Jessica had been thinking about Connor and Liam a lot — mostly about how she'd misjudged both of them completely — Lara believed her cousin. "Especially summer boys. I'd much rather celebrate girlhood. And us being the summer girls."

"I like that," Lara said, grinning. "Summer girls."

"Woo-hoo!" Jessica exclaimed, raising her tanned arms in the air.

And Greer happily gazed up at the showers of light. "See you next year, Pebble Beach!"

Lara smiled as everyone on their little section of beach burst into applause.

37

Jessica, waving good-bye, watched the two cars wend their way down the long driveway. Greer raised a nonchalant hand above her head, looking like a movie star, what with the silk scarf knotted around her hair. She was heading to the Canyon Ranch spa in the Berkshires for a mother-daughter weekend. She'd feigned indifference when she reported her destination, but Jessica knew exactly how much it meant to her. As Greer turned onto Peachtree Road, the Mercedes engine revved for a moment and the car took off in a cloud of dust.

Lara followed at a much more responsible speed, her black hair barely visible over the headrest of the mint-green VW Beetle. Uncle Frank owned a dealership in New Hampshire and had given Lara's mom an excellent price on the gently used car. Thanks to Ahoy, Lara had more than enough for her half, and so she splurged to have big purple flames painted on the sides. Greer had scoffed but Jessica loved it. It was so *Lara*. Lara honked her horn and blew Jessica a kiss.

When she was gone, Jessica slowly wandered through the living room, which somehow felt cozier than when she first walked in. The cupboard doors in the kitchen gaped open, displaying their emptied shelves. Her bags were stacked neatly in the hallway. Tucked inside her duffel was a pair of tiny white shorts — a parting gift from Greer. Though the present had made her smile, Jessica wasn't sure if she'd ever put them on again.

She had a few minutes to herself while her parents finished packing upstairs, so Jessica stepped onto the deck for one last look at the view. The brilliant, vivid blue of the cloudless sky. The deep-green forest edged with a crescent of muted yellow-tan sand. And dominating the scene — the steel-gray ocean flecked with silver waves. Jessica tried to burn the scene into her memory. It would be nine long months until she would see it again, but she definitely wasn't complaining.

Satisfied, she took her bags out to the car to wait for her parents. She glanced idly into the garage and something caught her eye. Connor's lacrosse stick leaned against the wall, a cobweb floating from the pocket. She'd been secretly hoping to run into him every day since Greer's revelation two weeks ago, but couldn't find the courage to actually call. Now she had an excuse.

Impulsively, she picked up the stick and jogged lightly down the road. When Connor's house emerged from behind the trees, she slowed. She stood outside cautiously, debating whether to just lean the stick against his door and go. She definitely didn't want to see Liam. But she forced herself to climb the flagstone steps and ring the bell. A blonde woman answered the door, her sun-bleached hair and shining eyes clearly establishing her as Connor's mom.

"May I help you?" she asked curiously.

"Hi, Mrs. Selden. Is Connor home? I'm his — I'm Jessica." It would be lying to say she was a friend, when she'd been anything but.

Mrs. Selden told her to wait and disappeared. A moment later, Connor appeared in the doorway and looked at Jessica strangely. "What are you doing here?"

Jessica held out the stick. "You left this at my house."

Connor stepped out and reached for the stick. "Thanks," he said shortly.

But Jessica didn't let go. "I need to ask you a question."

He let go, a look of scorn on his face. "I'll save you the trouble. Liam's down on the beach surfing. Bye." He turned away.

"That wasn't my question," Jessica said quietly, setting the stick on the ground and stepping backward. She knew she deserved his anger. She couldn't blame him if he refused to talk.

But he stopped. "What is it, then?"

She looked up at him from a few steps below. The difference in their heights made her feel small and unsure. "Do you still . . . like me?"

Connor just stared at her, confused.

"I didn't come here to see Liam. I came here to see you. To apologize." His look of surprise encouraged her to go on. "I'm sorry for using you. I'm especially sorry that I didn't realize how great of a friend you were to me. And I'm *really* sorry that I lost your friendship, because it was the best part of my summer." Jessica could hear the earnestness behind every word she spoke. She felt as if she'd been blind all summer — blind to how Connor felt about her. And . . . how she felt about him.

"Why are you telling me this now?" Connor asked with a trace of bitterness. "Because Liam's not interested?"

That hurt. As she formed her answer, Jessica tried to be as honest as possible — with him and with herself. "No, it's because we're leaving in a few minutes, and I didn't want to go without apologizing. And without telling you how I feel about you." Her heart pounded.

He looked down at her questioningly. "What are you talking about?"

"I like you," she said simply. "You're the only guy that I can just be myself with." She looked down at the fading lacrosse calluses on her palms. "I only recently realized how important that is."

"What made you realize it?" he asked disbelievingly. He stepped down toward her, keeping a careful distance.

Jessica met his eyes. They were her new favorite color — the same silver-gray of the ocean in Pebble Beach. "My family."

There was a heavy silence as she waited for Connor's answer. "I'll have to think about it," he said slowly. "It wasn't easy for me."

She nodded sadly. She hadn't expected instant forgiveness, but she didn't want to leave on bad terms. "I understand." She turned. It was time to go.

"Wait." He looked at her, and suddenly she could see his eyes blazing — had they always done that? How could she have missed it? Her heart lurched with regret for all the time she'd wasted.

"I'm so sorry, Connor," she whispered.

He stepped toward her slowly. "I just wish we had more time. You know, to talk."

"Could we start over next summer? Even just as friends?" Jessica asked hopefully.

He frowned, but his eyes sparkled. "Not if you plan to get better at lacrosse. It's hard on my ego."

She laughed. "No promises."

He flashed his goofy grin, the one she'd missed. "So, next summer, then . . ."

Seeing his smile again made her heart beat faster. She leaned forward to hug him good-bye. But instead of putting his arms around her shoulders, he took her face gently in his hands and kissed her softly, deeply. The world around her blurred.

Jessica closed her eyes, wishing the moment would last forever, knowing that she'd always remember this as a perfect summer.

READ ON FOR AN EXCERPT FROM

HotLanta

ANOTHER SIZZLING *Point* NOVEL

"Sydney! Sydney Duke! I need you downstairs, right now!"

The shrill sound of Sydney's mother's voice echoed all the way up her polished mahogany staircase, down the plush off-white carpeted hall, and right through the walls of Sydney's bedroom.

"I'm coming!" Sydney shouted back as she reluctantly earmarked the page she was reading in the latest issue of *Teen Vogue* and turned off the flat screen where the final minutes of her *Girlfriends* rerun was showing for the millionth time. She snatched up her hot-pink Marc Jacobs bag and matching jean jacket, even though Atlanta and the surrounding suburbs were still warm in late September. Nothing irked her more than when her mother yelled through the house like a wild banshee, but from the tone of her mother's voice, Sydney knew she needed to hurry downstairs and deal with whatever drama awaited before her ride arrived.

She had barely entered the kitchen before her mother started in on her. "Sweetie, I really think this time I may have found the perfect dress for you!"

"Honestly, Mom. The way you were screaming, I thought this was a life-threatening emergency." Sydney grabbed a handful of grapes from the crystal fruit bowl.

"This *is* an emergency. We only have a few weeks left, and Lord knows it'll take at least that long to find both you and your sister the perfect dresses."

"I suppose," Sydney sighed, leaning over her mother's

shoulder to glance at the dog-eared page of the October issue of *Vanity Fair* that lay open. "Um, as much as I love Roberto Cavalli's dresses for — I don't know — the MTV Awards, don't you think it's a bit flashy for your party?" she hinted none too subtly, after quickly perusing the over-the-top, beaded, strapless creation shown in the fashion layout. "How about a dress with a little understated elegance? Something more along the lines of Tracy Reese."

Her mother rolled her eyes. "Nothing about my twelve-year-anniversary party is going to be described as understated. And there's no way I, Keisha Duke, will allow either of my daughters to blend in with the crowd on such a big and very expensive night in honor of our family. So you can just forget about Tracy Reese."

"Mom," Sydney pleaded. "She's one of my favorite designers!"

"And that's fine, but the answer is still no. You can wave your little power-to-the-people fist and support black designers all you want when it's your event, but there's no way I'm going to let my friends think we suffer from everyday-people taste. Period." Keisha Duke rarely bothered to hide her need to keep way ahead of the Joneses. She flipped to another page and ran a finger over a picture showing a slinky black number with raw seams and a plunging neckline. "Well, what about Stella McCartney? She's couture and vegan."

Three quick beeps from Carmen's car horn sounded through the open bay windows. "I'll tell you what: Why don't you keep doing your research while I'm at my committee meeting?" Sydney broke for the front door. "Don't forget, I have a movie date with Marcus afterwards, so I might be home a little late."

"Marcus, Usher, Ne-Yo, or whomever you think you're in love with this week, I expect you home no later than one A.M., young lady. And tell Carmen this better be the last time she beeps any car horn in front of my house. This ain't the projects!"

"Yes, Mother," Sydney tossed over her shoulder, rushing toward freedom. She was more aware of that than anyone.

Despite the fact that it was almost seven o'clock, the sky was still fairly bright, and a soft Georgia breeze greeted Sydney as she stepped out the massive front door and ran down the marble steps of the Duke estate.

The sharp smell of newly cut grass burned inside her nose, as she waved hello to the workers dotting the front grounds. Like clockwork, they arrived every Friday afternoon to mow the lawn, trim the hedges, and tend to the exotic flowers that decorated the impressive three-acre property. Keisha Duke might have been a certified control freak when it came to keeping up appearances, but at the end of the day, everything she touched looked amazing. Their home was easily one of the most admired in the exclusive, multimillion-dollar Buckhead subdivision, if not in all of the surrounding Atlanta area.

"What's up, Syd?" Carmen asked as Sydney settled herself in her best friend's car. Since the day when they'd been lined up in height order and Carmen had been placed directly behind Sydney at their exclusive Montessori kindergarten orientation class, Carmen had been extremely comfortable being Sydney's faithful follower. The only place where Carmen didn't trace Sydney's footsteps was in all her charity work, which cut down a great deal of their one-on-one face time.

"Just happy to see the end of another busy week. Your timing is on point, as usual," Sydney said, fiddling with the XM radio.

Carmen pulled her birthday present — a black Land Rover Freelander — around the fountain and back down the Dukes' lengthy driveway.

"You think? It's almost seven. We're barely going to make the start of the meeting. I got caught up looking at the latest update on YoungRichandTriflin.com."

"Umm, I just don't know why you waste so much time reading YRT. You know that it's written by some hater who you probably don't even speak to and has nothing better to do than talk about people and their personal business," Sydney answered with a roll of her eyes. Recently, everyone in school had become obsessed with the scandalous blog started by an anonymous Brookhaven student. Every week all the latest news, trends, and hot gossip from the Atlanta region's most exclusive private high schools was broadcasted to everyone that logged on. Occasionally, if the gossip proved juicy enough, the site administrator would send out a special all-alert bulletin. Not that Sydney would ever admit it, but she too was totally addicted.

READ ON FOR AN EXCERPT FROM
THE *NEW YORK TIMES* BESTSELLER

SOUTH BEACH

ANOTHER JUICY *Point* NOVEL

"South Beach?" Alexa cut in. Now, there was tremor of excitement in her voice. "South Beach is supposed to be this amazing up-and-coming spring break spot. And I think it got written up in *Elle* as one of the world's sexiest getaways!" Holly heard Alexa rustling about in her room, most likely going through her giant stack of fashion magazines.

"Here it is," Alexa said after a minute, then read aloud: "'South Beach, Florida. The land of rhythm, rumba, and rum margaritas!'"

"Does it really say that?" Holly asked, laughing.

"Let me finish," Alexa said. "'South Beach is a glamorous, glitzy town with an unmistakable Latin flavor. SoBe, as it's commonly called, overflows with sandy beaches for sun-worshipping, and spicy clubs for dancing the night away.'" Alexa giggled with delight. "And there's this photo of the ritzy Rose Bar, in the Delano hotel. Holly, it sounds perfect! Let's do it."

Holly was overwhelmed. South Beach did sound appealing . . . and very grown-up. Holly was still unsure about Alexa, but going to Florida with her would definitely be an improvement over staying home with her entire family.

Holly could hear the clickety-clack of Alexa's fingers on a keyboard. "I'm on Orbitz right now. I can look up flights for Miami and —"

"Wait," Holly interrupted. This was moving way

too fast for her. "I need to think about it a little. And ask my grandmother if we can stay with her. *And* ask my parents if I can even go." She dreaded the mere thought of that.

"Okay," Alexa said. "You think, and take care of all the yucky permission stuff. Meanwhile, I'm going to find us cheap flights. Call me back!" Then she clicked off.

Holly remembered her childhood nickname for Alexa: "Little Miss Bossy." She wondered how that aspect of Alexa's personality might play out on their trip — if they did end up going.

Holly snapped her phone shut and stretched across her twin bed. She looked at the framed photo that hung above the bed, of her, Meghan, and Jess. Sweaty and triumphant after a track meet, they stood with their arms around one another's shoulders. Holly's friends would probably freak if she told them she was going away with Alexa. They thought of Alexa and her impeccably dressed crowd as total snobs.

But now that the kernel of Miami Beach was in Holly's head, she could feel it expanding and growing, taking the shape of reality.

If Holly was being completely honest with herself, her desire to go to Miami had something to do with a boy. The boy she'd met down there, three years ago. Holly felt a flush climbing her neck into her face. She hadn't thought about Diego in a while. But talking about Florida had triggered all the old memories. They rushed back now, as vivid as ever.

Diego Felipe Mendieta. He'd been fourteen at the time, but tall for his age. His skin was the color of cocoa butter, his eyes were black as olives, and his hair was dark and glossy. Whenever he smiled, the two deepest, most adorable dimples appeared in his cheeks. Diego lived in her grandmother's apartment building and he'd introduced himself in the lobby one day, which had absolutely floored Holly. Boys like Diego never talked to her. But the two of them had ended up spending the whole week together — surfing on Haulover Beach, bike-riding north to Sunny Isles, eating triple-scoop ice-cream cones on the boardwalk. Then, on Holly's last night, Diego had given Holly her first — and, so far, only — kiss.

Holly closed her eyes, summoning that one yummy memory. It had been around ten o'clock, a muggy, sticky Miami night. She and Diego had gotten choco-late chip ice-cream cones, and decided to bring them down to the beach. The full moon had cast its pale reflection on the surface of the ocean. Holly remem-bered the feel of the cold ice cream on her tongue and the foamy water on her bare toes. She and Diego had fallen silent, gazing up in wonder at the moon, and Holly had felt an odd shift between them — a kind of electric spark. She'd never felt that happen with a boy before. And she'd suddenly become aware of Diego's arm so close to hers. She'd resisted the urge to touch him — to rest her hand on the sleeve of his T-shirt — but then Diego had touched *her*. He leaned over, brought his fingers to her lips, and lightly wiped the corner of Holly's mouth.

"Ice cream," he explained with a half smile. Holly wanted to die of mortification, but before she could, Diego kissed her. Really kissed her. The fullness of his lips and the salty-sweet taste of his mouth, and his warm hand on her waist made Holly's knees wobble. She almost dropped her cone in the sand. Kissing was so much better than Holly had ever imagined — soft and warm and easy. She'd wanted the kiss to last forever, but Diego had gently ended it, smiled at Holly, and turned back to the ocean. Still, when they'd gone back up to the boardwalk, their fingers had brushed together as if they were about to hold hands. And when they parted ways in the elevator, Diego had given her another kiss, this time on the cheek, and promised to stay in touch.

And they had, Holly remembered as she lay on her bed. They'd e-mailed and IMed for the rest of the summer and into the school year, trading reminisces about their week in Miami. Holly remembered how her heart would bang against her ribs whenever she saw his name pop up on her screen. But, as the year went on, their correspondence had petered out. After some time, Diego faded in Holly's mind, remaining a blissful, if distant, memory.

Holly opened her eyes and swung her legs off the bed. She looked at herself in the round mirror above her desk. Her green-gray eyes were very bright and her freckled cheeks dark pink. Holly *had* sometimes teased herself with the thought that she'd go back to Miami Beach one day and have a romantic reunion with Diego. But she'd gotten so busy with schoolwork and track, and sports camp in the summer, that there hadn't been another chance to visit Grandma Ida.

Until now.

To Do List:
Read all the Point books!

Airhead
Being Nikki
By **Meg Cabot**

Suite Scarlett
By **Maureen Johnson**

Sea Change
The Year My Sister Got Lucky
South Beach
French Kiss
Hollywood Hills
By **Aimee Friedman**

And Then Everything
Unraveled
By **Jennifer Sturman**

The Heartbreakers
The Crushes
By **Pamela Wells**

This Book Isn't Fat,
It's Fabulous
By **Nina Beck**

Wherever Nina Lies
By **Lynn Weingarten**

Summer Girls
Summer Boys
Next Summer
After Summer
Last Summer
By **Hailey Abbott**

In or Out
By Claudia Gabel
In or Out
Loves Me, Loves Me Not
Sweet and Vicious
Friends Close,
Enemies Closer